METYMPSYCHOSIS

WRITTEN BY
CHRIS KELSO

ILLUSTRATIONS BY
EDGING ON DEATH

FERAL DOVE
MAINE
PHILADELPHIA
2025

TABLE OF CONTENTS

INTRODUCTION

CREATURELINESS AND THE
HYPER-SENSITIVE DEATH

STORY

METYMPSYCHOSIS
PARTS 1 & 2
(FEATURING EDGINGONDEATH)

BONUS

ON SYMBIOSIS AND THE WELCOME LIMITATIONS
OF COLLABORATION
(FEATURING DENNIS COOPER)

Creatureliness and the Hyper-sensitive Death
An introduction by the author

Metympsychosis is a book of two modes – on the one hand it actively rallies against the state of denial, but in another way the book is a quest for a lie. Our protagonist Eadie knows his inner mechanisms are creaking, that his 'self' demands change of some description, but he initially believes he can achieve satisfaction by simply forgetting his old life. This new position of amnesia will keep Eadie at a safer distance from his own death. Of course, he comes to discover that true rebirth is a gruelling, agonising process – a transformation which might bring him closer to death and his own ugliness than he has ever comfortably been before.

In Ernest Becker's opus of psychophilosophical thought, *The Denial of Death*, he explores the paradoxical nature of man's place in the world and his experiential suffering during a true mind/body transformation. He reminds us that *"full humanness means full fear and trembling, at least some of the waking day."* Even when Eadie has had his grandmother executed and he succumbs his physical body to antemortem deterioration, the terror (or the 'creatureliness') remains intact.

Eadie, in leaving behind his thuggish past, has successfully achieved what Kierkegaard referred to as 'the lie of character'. But, having accomplished unfreedom and untruth, Eadie finds he is still unhappy. Death continues to plague him. He longs for the final movement, that which may see him penetrate the real and become a god. A self-realised soul. But Eadie cannot generate this movement on his own. He needs the visitor to frighten him into triggering *a new causa sui project*. Ironically, the visitor is a shadow of death himself. Eadie unintentionally makes an ultra-sensitive animal of himself. When discussing schizophrenia, Becker described hyper-sensitive individuals as the 'cursed animals' of evolution.

The character looks to rebirth himself into unrepressed madness with full physical and psychic expansiveness, but with the shell and instincts of a majestic insect. The best way to keep death at bay is to own it in some way. Eadie does not realise the nightmare that is the life of a hyper-sensitive insect. He possesses all the same hang-ups and self-awareness of a human being, a terrible knowledge of the complex symbol of death, but percolated through an alien body with its own separate organic demands. Remember, our bodies are problems which demand explanation. Man possesses a definitive body with inner burdens and its own environmental design. Unlike the caterpillar which becomes the butterfly, our transformation requires physical and mental upheaval. We are anchored in awareness. When the body folds and warps, we feel it. We consider what we see before us. The fat and sleepy caterpillar is under biological hypnosis. It considers nothing. Eadie plays with the risk of evolution in a way that cannot end favourably for him. His ignorance, his depression and denial, all keep him from considering the true consequences of transformation. We are simultaneously gods and worms, or as Maslow would describe 'gods with anuses'. Becker explains, *"What does it mean to be born again for man? It means for the first time to be subjected to the terrifying paradox of the human condition, since one must be born not as a god, but as a man, or as a god-worm, or a god who shits."* So, the result is always the same, even in this final stage. Even after successful forgetting.

Man's character is a neurotic structure and the recycling process is inevitably painful, physically and psychologically. The body breaks down but so too will our strategies for avoiding the awful real — those precious tools of repression (which help us deal with the complex symbol of death) are rendered useless. Eadie will suffer the greatest nightmare of all. A hyper-sensitive death.

PART
ONE

1.

The young team stands over Eadie Daly's grandmother with huge, jagged stones that look like meteorite fragments cupped in their hands. Mikey, Squareheid, MacLean are beshadowed in the clearing like a trio of gunfighters in a stand-off. Their leader, Bible Johnny, lurks in the distance, ready to give the final instruction. It's a Tuesday. How the fuck has it come to this? He asks himself. Well, the bad memories had persisted and Eadie was at his wits end. He'd brought the boys here as a last throw of the dice. The only way to get rid of his old life was to kill the woman he loved most in the world. Times are changed; we also are changed with them.

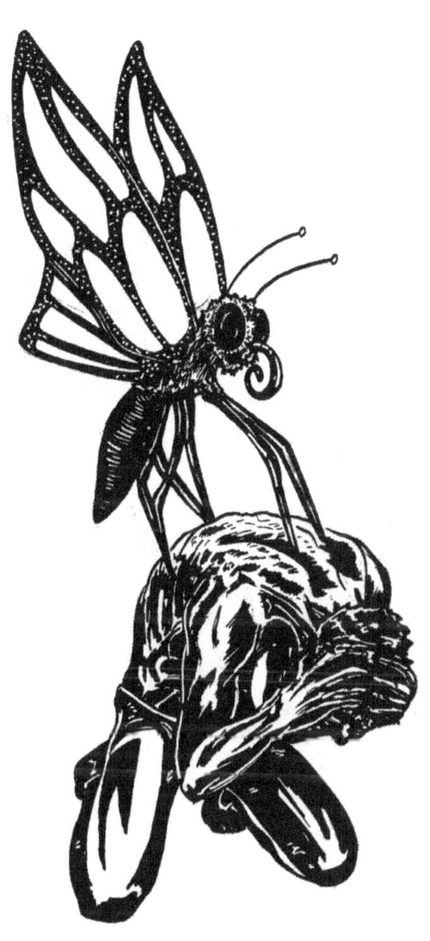

2.

In The Zhuangzi, Daoist philosopher Zhuangzi Zhuang wrote of a man (also called Zhuang Zhou) who dreamt he was a butterfly. In the dream, Zhuang Zhou believed he was a butterfly, had always been a butterfly, and all memory of another persona had dissipated into the swirling oneiric ether. The butterfly fell and the dream faded - Zhuang Zhou awoke to find himself a lowly human again. Was he a human who dreamt he was a butterfly, or a butterfly dreaming he was Zhou? Zhuang Zhou had been touched by a profound precognitive dream, a feeling that would not abate. The dream had saturated him in its glorious filtrate. He was reminded that he could be somewhere else. That one day he would be somewhere else again, and the dream of his human form would become a dream in itself, or better yet, a faded memory.

Was Eadie an upstanding citizen who dreamt he was a hooligan, or a sleeping hooligan dreaming he was an upstanding citizen? He had recollections of wading through effluent middens and rain-sodden streets with gangs of boys, enacting some kind of psuedosnuff theatre. It was all amateur dramatics empty of any real philosophy, but it wasn't a dream. He remembers never brushing his teeth properly. Biting at dirt-encrusted fingernails. Jagging and snorting, enduring cocaine jaw. Kicking cans. Giving and receiving dead arms. Flayed knees. Entrails over a chain-link fence. Broken pinkies under a pileup. Shattered windows. Too-loud-music and a torso crumpled with laughter. A regional accent. Small stadiums with balding grass. Woodsmoke in the air. No emotional vocabulary. No hope and, for a time, fucking loving it. The thought of it all always turned to vapour. All of Eadie's pubic hair fell out that morning. He held the wiry clumps in his hands and would've felt like Dionysus beholding a rake of rough bindweed had he any prior knowledge of Greek mythology.

There was a time between all the madness and murder. The mechanisms of transformation started churning one night when he heard foreign footsteps in his flat. Shoeless feet crept about, gently padding across the polyester carpet. A floorboard creaked beneath faint pressure confirming the presence as unequivocally real. Eadie was assaulted by a screed of runes which scanned across his field of vision – alchemical symbols written in a dead dream language. Meaningless and silent, but somehow vital. No one ever spoke a breath. Eadie had never seen anyone, either. He never touched the watcher's flesh with his own. Yet, as the visitations continued, the weight of another presence in the room scratched Eadie's scalp with dull needlepoints of dread. There was a smell - organic molecules soured to the tune of rusted rebar. Every day that week he'd felt it. Heard it. Smelt it. Been molested by its patient secret.

***

Stalking the murky darkness of his halfway-swanky apartment was just a bad memory. Something unlocked, willing into presence, and just begging to be fucking remembered. The flash of hieroglyphs ceased and Eadie was left in blackness to contemplate the dream-prisoner looming over him. He felt it's ache for acknowledgement but remained tight in a crushed ball of mock slumber ....

The dream triggers the first phase — pupal stage until fate intervenes. The the 'inter-mortum stage'. runes are the same images a Reincarnation is a result of a caterpillar sees flashing across the shuddering inner-movement, an inside of its silken chrysalis. inside death. Specimen hidden in The taste of rapid cell-growth.

.... refusing to let the brain-barriers down for even a second.

Its breath was ragged, the wriggling shadow of clawed fingers extended towards him, darkening the multicoloured veins throbbing on the underside of his eyelids. As a terrified gasp escaped him, he never opened his eyes. If he kept them closed, knowing day would eventually come and he would wake up unharmed.

Day always came.

On the fourth day of these visitations, there was no sun. A dim natural light exposed the fractured plumb line of the town from his window. Eadie peeled his body from the couch and observed the sodden impression of himself on the soft leather. He'd urinated his trousers. Chewed an ulcer into his left cheek until his mouth filled with the copper aura of blood. He had a feeling in his bowels that he was being robbed of his haecceity. This could not continue. Drastic action was necessary.

3.

A week before the visitations, Eadie had stood on the pier. The surf kissed the shoal, looked like a soft, inviting blanket. He thought about how far he'd come and how much he'd achieved, yet every day he wondered will today really be the day I walk into the sea?

Everything sung in favour of suicide. Eadie's great-grandfather had committed suicide in the family home. No one really spoke about it, but it happened. His Gran revealed it one night after one too many Taliskers. On the pier, the bad memories were everywhere but they hadn't yet manifested as creatures of the night. The essential organic tools were in place, though; the inner technology of sadness would summon and make animate Eadie's forgotten life.

The world before Eadie's corporate life seemed like a false memory. He'd been a junkie, considerably unemployed. Hanging around in gangs with local lunatics like Bible Johnny and his young team MacLean, Mikey, and Squareheid[1]. Now he had money, a career, a pension, but his body was deteriorating at a supernatural rate. The skeleton seemed to grow underneath, but the skinsuit stayed the same size, becoming too tight around the edges. Maybe it was the residue of guilt from his old life that pulled him to water. One final baptism. With each passing day Eadie's flesh pulled taut over wide, sharp crests of bone, to the point of near perforation. Vessels snaked between valleys of meat and pulp. His eyeballs bugged out in a ridiculous insect-gawk. Then his pubes falling out? It must have had something to do with his job.

---

[1] *In the South there were the South Team, the San Toi, Bastard Powery, and the Bingo-Bango Boys. The Norman Conks ruled the East End while the North was Uppy Mad Squad and Tongs territory. Eadie and his pals were in the smaller outcropping of the Conks called No-Men Squad. They were animals.*

The air was brassy, sulfidic. Suicide weather. A leviathan appeared in the distance, but Eadie wasn't perturbed. The great ridges of its spine wounded the doom-clouds above. He let it pass into the dark ulterior powers of the sea, almost smiling. Eadie decided he wouldn't let the water take him just yet. Not in this weather. Not when the great local Goliaths continued to strike a note of beauty in his heart. Not when he continued to occupy a stark bewilderment when recollecting his former passions. He'd come so far from that suicidal fuck-up but it haunted him in a way that felt malevolent.

Eadie glided along the promenade like a miserly apparition, accepting only the raw atmospheric quiet which engulfed him. Little jagged blades of rain nicked his face and he let it. He enjoyed the hissing in his ears and the nibbling drips like a thousand insect bites – as it happened he was also being molested by angry aphids. The weather seemed, at least, to consider him. Made mark to respond to him, to treat him like he existed if only to be maimed by its falling water. It was immensely sympathetic. In this singular moment Eadie believed in goodness. He was the only person on the promenade. The weather made rough love to his personage, and he let it. He decided to go back home. Eadie started to think being Scottish was a restriction, that any allegiance to nationality was narrowing. Why was he outside anyway?

4.

His fingernails started to peel off. Eadie sought help from a man who lived in the big high rises in the blotted-out part of town. Davie used to be a fabricator in the old town, which was dominated by engineering works and pop-up industrial units devoted to community commerce. Eadie's grandpa had known Davie from the assembly line days. Then the factory shut down and Davie, lacking in life experience or formal education, found himself awoken in a new nightmare of poverty and drugs. He had always been an amnesiologist. He didn't charge people and there was no exploitation or showmanship. No spectacle. Davie saw his work as a service. But there were still people who believed he was an evil wizard of sorts.

The council schemes and high rises produced the best amnesiologists. Living in the shadows gave people in the effaced regions extrasensory gifts, at least that was the rumour. Eadie knew this world well, originally hailing from an estate not far from the abandoned knitwear factory. Not quite the darkest part of town, but still grimly sunless with soul-fucked streets. It occurred to him he hadn't been in the darkness since he was a teenager.

The elevator doors were a canvas of hateful cacography, as indecipherable as the runes[2] etched across the backs of his eyelids each night. There was a ding, and the lift exposed its caged enclosure, which narrowed into a mile-deep dark. The lift shuddered and began to rise. Restless ghosts moaned in the shaftway.

---

[2] *Hatred had evolved since the primitive days of the sectarian Penny Mobs and razor gangs. Their ideology was less fascistic and broad. They were agents of parochial psychodramas. There was a simulacra of terrorism. That was a different time, a different country. A different universe.*

Chittering football commentary blared from the hall. He chapped on Davie's door and a dog barked. The jangle of locks, chains, and bolts unfastening lasted for about 30 seconds until Davie's face peered round the side of the door. Heavy, doleful eyes caught Eadie's and the man gave a silent insomniac hello. Davie turned away, leaving the door ajar, and Eadie pushed his way into the house. The place was a vision of neglect. Newspapers were stacked in great towers throughout the hallways and there was an overwhelming stench of general decline. Incalculable equations and symbols adorned the peeling 70's wallpaper.

In the living room Davie sat on a couch, cotton birthing itself from burst upholstery. The television blared with foreign commentary that sounded like one sustained note of white noises. Davie turned down the volume. There was a small cassette player on a TV tray beside the couch and from it the rabid barks emanated. Davie squashed his finger over the stop button and the dogs went silent. He muted the commentary static and smiled gloomily. Davie addressed Eadie in a soft even-keeled murmur with a mouthful of black, broken teeth. His big wet eyes also alluded to a poisoned bloodstream.

"NEED TO MAKE SURE THE NEIGHBOURS DON'T HEAR OUR CONVERSATIONS. NOSEY BASTARDS HAVE ALWAYS GOT THEIR EARS TO THE WALL."

"Can you help me forget?"

"FORGET? LISTEN, SON, YOU'VE NO IDEA THE BURIED MEMORIES YOU'VE GOT IN THAT HEAD OF YOURS. YOU'VE HAD AT LEAST THREE LIVES. MAYBE MORE."

"I'm having visitations."

"MMHM."

He squinted one eye at Eadie as if in assessment of his character.

"NOT UNUSUAL. YOU MUST BE DUE ANOTHER AWAKENING.
YOUR BODY LOOKS DONE-IN, SON.
IT'S READY TO SHED"

"Another awakening?"

"YOU A DRINKER, SON?"

Davie's rotten teeth puzzled together in a hideous smile.

"No, teetotaller"

"TO GET RID OF THIS THING YOU'LL NEED YOUR IMAGINATION, SO GET DRINKING ASAP" – Davie finally unsquinted – "PLATO BELIEVED THE LIVER WAS THE SOURCE OF ALL IMAGINATION. THE BIOLOGICAL SEAT OF ALL DREAMS[3]"

Davie got up from his chair making a sound like a tennis player in full serve and reached into a cardboard box full of notepads and paper. He plucked out a yellowed diary and handed it to Eadie. Eadie observed the offering. 'The Journal of Boab Daly'.

"This was my great grandpa's journal?"

Davie nodded. Eadie fingered the rough cover and peeled it open to the first page.

---

[3] *Plato claimed images received by the liver (from the intellect) kept evil desires at bay, offering the body's primary/sole source of divination. Amnesiologists in backwater Scottish towns blindly believed that alcohol stimulated the organ and heightened the intensity and vividness of the intellect's secret imagery.*

I cannot remember why I was on the run or from what memory but I had the pace of a skelped fox which suggests I had done something worth forgetting.

To many' my character lies rank among the lazy sugs and mince minded of this world. You may see me in a similar light if judgment is a characteristic dominant to your sensibility. Needless to say' my life has been governed by a singular purpose seeking out islands of respite after extended periods of vagrancy and transgression. Having shambled across the scheme lands avoiding factory labour' spending twenty four sleepless hours journeying in haunted freight cabooses. I believed my very bones had become more marsh than marrow. It would not be an exaggeration to say that my hair had been eternally impressioned by dirt' and that my immortal soul had been plugged with so much engine smoke a pit boss could've enslaved my holy spirit as a mine canary. Suffice to say the dust of many miles hung upon me. I didn't know it but I was looking to forget and escape a memory or a feeling which was in hot pursuit.

Eadie closed the journal and looked at Davie with a bewildered expression.

"Why do you have this?"

"BOAB GAVE IT TO ME."

"Why?"

"NO IDEA" - Davie squinted again and an impish grin broadened his face. - **"PEOPLE WITH HOLES IN THEIR MEMORIES DO ODD THINGS SOMETIMES."**

"He came to you to forget?"

Davie nodded, still smiling.

"There was a rumour about my great-grandpa Boab. Everyone in my family blamed him for the way we were. Fuck-ups, you know?"

"I CAN'T BREAK CLIENT CONFIDENTIALITY, SON, SO END YER FISHIN'"

He reached into his rotten maw and pulled out a shrunken black tooth, stripped of enamel but sprigged with withered nerve endings. It came loose with remarkable, disturbing ease. Eadie held his stomach. Noticing Eadie's revulsion, Davie stuck the tooth down the side of the couch like a child lazily dispensing with a loose sweet wrapper.

"He killed himself just after my gran was born."

"HE DID."

"My mum said that was what triggered it all. The drugs and trauma in the family. Fuck knows."

"MMHM."

"I'm interested in building a wall. There's a memory I've tried to bury and it's coming after me. stalking me at night. It won't leave me the fuck alone. I feel myself...changing. something wants me to change. Do you think something wants me to change again?"

Davie nodded to the journal.

"READ THAT FIRST. PART OF THE CLEANING PROCESS IS INTERPRETATION. THE SKEPTICAL BRAIN NEEDS TO BELIEVE IT CAME TO ITS OWN CONCLUSIONS. THIS IS YOUR LINK TO ME. READ IT, INTERPRET IT. YOU'LL KNOW WHAT TO DO ONCE YOU GET TO THE END."

Eadie held the book in his hand, feeling the coarse leather.

"I thought you were going to put a sci-fi headset on me or something. Wave a wand. Make me drink a potion."

"NAH. AMNESIOLOGIST IS MORE SUBTLE AND PHILOSOPHICAL THAN THAT, SON. I'M MORE A GUIDE THAN A PLAGUE DOCTOR."

Davie gestured to a bleeding needle and dropper on the coffee table, surrounded by articles of shite. Eadie didn't touch the stuff anymore and he ricocheted a forlorn, empty glance from Davie's gaze to the waste-strewn floor. Davie shrugged, pressed the remote and the football commentary resumed its previous din. He made that strained tennis-player noise again as he reached for the paraphernalia and Eadie knew it was time to leave.

"BEFORE YOU GO, NIP INTO THE SHOPS AND GET YOURSELF A BOTTLE OF TALISKER OR SOME BEER. TIME TO ENGAGE WITH YOUR BODY, SON. IT'S TRYING TO TELL YOU SOMETHING. AND REMEMBER, THE ANTIDOTE TO THE CORPORATE INFECTION IS SACRIFICE."

"Thank you for this…"

Eadie glanced at the notebook in his hands.

"YOU KNOW, THERE ARE PEOPLE WHO THINK I'M A BOGUS NECROMANCER, THAT I GIVE PEOPLE THE WRONG INFORMATION. THAT I EAT PEOPLE'S SOULS."

"I'm desperate enough to trust you."

A voice asked him with awful quiddity in its tone:

"Have you ever thought
about the shared secrets
you hold beneath
your skin?"

That night, the visitor unzipped Eadie's skin, yanking it past the arcs of his skull and down over the length of his abdomen with a wet, leather-like squeak. One final tug freed the suit from around his buckled knees and Eadie was finally naked, dissected in Gross Anatomy. The figure stood in silhouette, clutching the skin-suit like a punctured jellyfish. The air stung his exposed striated muscles. He couldn't talk. He couldn't breathe. His brain tried to comprehend the situation but the reality was too shocking, it could not be untangled from his wildest sensorial nightmare. The visitor dropped the hunk of damp tissue to the floor and explained in symbols that his mask was slipping. Was the visitor his future-self looking back through the funnel of his past? Davie talked about Eadie's past 'lives,' plural. What the fuck did that mean?

"Do you even know what's beneath
your own skin?
Have you ever
looked?"

"No."

"There could be
anything.
You'll never know
until you look.
Complex knowledge
hidden beneath tesseracts of intestines."

5.

He had memories of one past life, a time when he lived for multi-coloured stimulants and anxiety-suppressants, for heavy music and street women, the lure of the starving night. Now, sat with the tumbler of Talisker in his shaking hand, he could barely keep down a swallow of alcohol.

There was the lazy Wednesday after a night of gigging and drinking and drugging and fucking and denial. He was good at denial. It was a hereditary quality. The Daly's were a rough family, everyone except his saint-like granny. Mum and dad were the addicts. He was in care by age six. Experimenting with booze and hash at eleven. Sexually active by twelve. Abused by thirteen. Given a gang by fourteen. He inverted the denial like they had taught him. Let the corporation tamp out the honest fire within his gut, build him a tin-ear. A personality his grandmother could love. And now he loved his grandmother in return. Or he assumed he did. Thick darkness approached from the schemes and Eadie opened up his great-grandpa Boab's journal, hoping to glean some knowledge before the visitor arrived again. He took a sip of the whiskey and shuddered as an old voice sang into the great flapping flexagon of his heartbox.

sunday morning, March:

I found myself trapped in a strange nameless pocket of land. A place with no welcome sign. A town forgotten for its quiet ghosts and deceased roads. It's common knowledge that if you go a wandering in these parts, the small towns therein will get you. You will be sucked into strange situations and changed forever. The wandering life is sometimes like a woman, beautiful and caressing, and draggled and stabbing all at once, and friendship and generosity are opiates concealed from strangers in this place. I write, not to bore you with sanctimonious knowledge, but to inform, and to give the treatment.

I headed northwest on the railway ties straight toward that part of the country crudely marked "NO ENTRY" on the map. I was deep in the belly of the dead towns, but transport remained regular, so I needn't have succumbed to anxiety. That's when I happened upon the nameless town and the great lepidopterarium presented itself.

Monday:

I am leaving the factories. Sunset found me in a forest cleared of its pine. The noname town was a memory of its own. I started for a meal and lodging at a small white slum hut half a mile ahead just by the abandoned track. To think years ago I was tossing chips into an old Hinkley insider up. I was working for an engineer by the name of Dean Burnie III. Burnie was considered as good a man as there was on the road: careful' yet fearless' kindhearted' yet impulsive' a man whose friends would fight for him and whose enemies hated him right royally. Burnie would wind up homeless and liminal like me. A casualty of dead labour. The roads got him in the end. He killed himself claiming he could not watch the future visions of himself commit atrocities. I looked at the wasted forest and wondered if a clumsy giant had passed through. I prepared a speech for the proprietor' a speech to this effect:

"I am the liminal dreamvendor' sole active member of the ancient brotherhood of the troubadours. It is against the rules of our order to receive money. We have the habit of asking a night's lodging in exchange for repeating verses and fairy tales."

Eadie thought about his understanding of 'liminality'. Everyone used that word to describe being 'in between'. What did it mean that his grandfather was a liminal dream-vendor? This sounded pretentious and fanciful, traits his family would never tolerate in one of their own. The way his great-grandfather spoke was different as well. Ancient and literate. The 'wandering life' was something he related to. Both men were fugitives of memory in a way. He knew Dean Burnie III's grandson, Bryan, who was Bible Johnny's estranged dad, but the kind-heartedness wasn't hereditary. The past, present, and future seemed to bleed together in a fourth-dimensional triptych. Eadie read on:

As I approached the dwelling the speech passed from my memory and sieved into the void of forgotten thought. I moved to the side gate to appeal to the old fern tickled slumghost enthroned ominously in the porch rocker. Before I could utter a syllable' her son' the property owner' lifted his wet dandelion head from behind the disc of a large dog bowl. He shall ever be named the dogman herein. The miceminded dogman had an inscrutable countenance and refused me a place in his kennel. Neither would he share his offal. Apparently he used to be someone else before he was a dog. The slumghost on the porch rose to assure me in a whanging yelp that they did not take "nobody in under no circumstances." Then the dogman' somewhat placated by my 'liminal' expression' steered his thumb in the direction of the woods' saying: "There is a sug in there who will take you in sure." I asked if this sug kept watchdogs. He assured me the neighbour had no need for such a precaution.

Rumours and hearsay of a man who lived as a dog were not uncommon and most schemes had their own incarnation of the archetype, a man who walked around on all fours and ate chum. People considered the dog-man an embarrassment, but he was a poet of the torture chamber, an artist of empathy and modesty. He asked nothing of anyone and lived on the streets until he died at the age of 102-years-old. He died on the streets and people told their kids to step over his body if they came across it.

The night with the sug around the corner was like a chapter from that curious document' "The Gospel according to st. John." It transpires that he "could not afford to turn a man away" because once he slept three nights in the rain when he walked here from an unknowable Ayrshire town. No one would give him shelter. Wounded by the brotherlessness of his fellow man the sug decided that when he had a roof' he would go shares with whoever asked. Some strangers were good' some bad' but he would risk them all. His real name and address are of some consequence' but let us say he fits the description of a being called 'D'. An Amnesiologist. A professional forgetter. I found later that there were thousands like him. For the sake of argument let us call him "The Man Under the Yoke."

D was a sight. Lean as an old smackhead' sooty as a pair of coal tongs. Teeth black as all fuck. His Egyptian mummy jaws had a two weeks' beard. His shirt had not been washed since the flood. His ankles were innocent of socks. His hat was bandless.

It was surely impossible this was Davie, as he didn't look a day over sixty-five. The journal was dredging up more questions than answers and Eadie's patience was ebbing. It was comforting to see his great-grandfather go through similar trials, but he knew the ending. Boaby hung himself in the family home. Eadie's grandmother found the body. She'd been profoundly fucked up by it and committed herself to an agoraphobic existence thereafter.

Eadie thought about how he could become a better person. How would he ever atone for the wrongs he'd perpetrated? He had indulged in the most selfish and noxious deeds. Sitting there, reading the journal, choking down Talisker, he thought he was better now, enlightened in a sense, but was reluctant to spin his own redemption arc. In a way, the corporatisation of his life had imposed that improvement. The expectations of workplace etiquette were cutthroat and borderline Orwellian, yet he could not deny the improvement to his external environs. He was as far away as possible from people like the dog-man and the boy he was whilst in the young team, but it wasn't enough. He couldn't just run away from the visitor. But facing it could lead to complete annihilation. Already Eadie had decided that this was his great-grandpa's message. This was his early interpretation.

6.

Night came and so did the visitor. More questions. The runes made sense and the replies came from inside his own head. A new personality occupying the space between his ears.

"You've got
it all wrong.
It's the flesh that stifles the soul.
Confuses it, pollutes and infects it.
The soul has to be free.
Flesh is all just a lie."

"You believe in a soul.
You're here in front of me
with those desperate,
wet eyes.
You believe in a soul."

It fingered through his grandpa's journal and Eadie heard the book thoughtlessly hit the floor with a dull polyester-thud. He curled up drunk, like a post-mature foetus, and waited out the experience. The runes appeared printed across the clenched canvas of his eyelids. Then something more significant.

The 'Pascens stage'
is delayed because the subject does not have
a high-caloric intake.
This phase must be induced by a third party.

One must instil the hunger in the subject first.
If the subject does not have
an inclination
towards fatty foodstuffs, proteins, carbohydrates, alkaloids,
then matriphagy is the only alternative —
the only meal that can prepare
the budding larvae
for the
moulting phase.
In the absence of a mother
then the surrogate parent will suffice.
In this case a grandmother.

—a long ice-pick delicately traced the course of his cheek leaving a tear of blood in its wake.

This was the first contact he'd had with the visitor. Soon it would make complete contact with his life. It would find a way to absorb him.

Grandmother's death
will provide the inner movement
and her corpse
will provide sustenance and nutritional reserve
for the final metamorphosis.

Eadie slept in an envelope of silence. The corporate sedative of obfuscation, the relentless contradictions of synergy and data-moating, had eliminated all individual thought within and he used to sleep like the dead. But now he was back to the old sleeping patterns. He saw every hour.

***

At work, he drank luxury bottled water and watched the meniscus twinkle. He never felt like he deserved the expensive liquid. The corporate world was a strange lover. The company offered him a way out of his working-class hell so he couldn't very well turn it down. He was just so tired of being skint, of being high all the time. He'd felt alive with music and connected to a community, sure, but he couldn't survive and that in a way felt like hell. The corporation offered a way out without a university degree. He'd been scooped up by the notorious mass recruitment drive of 88[4]. The corporation gave work to thousands of down on their luck slum rats. But he soon learned that his employment was far from altruistic. The corporation gave him comfort but demanded his soul and his sanity. Eadie's life was a landfill of pressure and free-floating anxiety. He could never shed those apprehensions ever again. It was in his bloodstream. It was dispiriting and heartening to know he could never fully return to his old self because of this terminal infection.

---

4 *Modest Futures Foundation is an independent, for-profit organisation established with a preliminary £__________million endowment from the Sleeping Assets Scheme to improve employment outcomes for deprived people from marginalised backgrounds. The Foundation has successfully narrowed employment gaps by investing in evidence generation and improvement.*

***

He got ready for work. Filled his company planner, packed himself a sad, small lunch of a salad sandwich and an article of fruit and he ironed his shirt until it resembled a stretched sheet of pin-striped lead. Eadie looked at his fancy conapt set in antiseptic white with the occasional, yet tasteful, flourish of understated chromatism, and noticed the twinge of satisfaction diminishing within him.

***

On his lunchbreak, Eadie popped into the local artisan coffee shop called Le Mec. He was exhausted and couldn't succumb to the nauseated aversion growing inside him anymore. He needed coffee. When they gentrified this part of town the planners repurposed a lot of the old shops. Inside he saw a face he recognised. Le Mec used to be a greengrocers. Eadie's eyes caught a ghost from the past summoned from somewhere in his repressed dream world. It was Johnny Bible, formerly Jonathan Burnie, sitting at a bistro table delicately sipping froth from a demitasse mug. He seemed disarmingly neutered and non-threatening. Eadie was compelled to approach him. The movement inside him begged to reconnect.

"Johnny?"

Johnny Bible lowered his mug. The serious and suspicious teenager he once was contorted the surface of his physiognomy in a way that was darkly familiar. Eadie pulled out the seat opposite and sat down.

"How you been keeping?"

Johnny put down his latte and knitted his brow.

Johnny smiled bleakly.

He was a perfect illustration of the lazy and mince-minded sugs from his great-grandpa's diary. The enlightened spirit in Eadie recoiled at the word 'poof,' but he had a history with this man, and he felt relevant to what was happening to him. An ingredient of that inner movement.

Johnny looked at him as if he had three heads. His torso was twisted, wide, sharply quadrilateral. Yet his mouth was a slit, his speech slow and slurred by the too-big tongue locked inside.

Eadie had a good job now. Johnny couldn't understand. The recruitment drive didn't get as far as his scheme, but that's life. Johnny wouldn't have spared a second thought if Purefake had come calling for him. Christ, it wasn't Eadie's fault he got out. He had relinquished all his passions to the corporation with a surprising readiness. But that's called commitment. Now he made Purefake[5] Skins for a living and he staked his claim to a single mote of the sunshine's divine light. Johnny took a step forward, his chair screeching in a way that silenced the middle-class murmur of Le Mec's clientele. His nose touched Eadie's chin. His eyes were slanted, mucus-encrusted chrysalides.

---

[5] *Purefake was the leading fraud bot manufacturer in the country. The money on offer was also much better than that of other software application companies. Eadie only worked in skin-design but he held other areas of responsibility: farm duties related to the incorporation of more complex software functionality. Whatever that meant. He was being upskilled and even considered for promotion. There was excitement in the prospect of promotion and in this sense the corporation had won.*

"I can be here. Every fucking right."

Eadie noted the fart-smell of beer on Johnny's breath, despite his recent supping forth from an overpriced coffee.

"I know, man. I'm not saying you shouldn't be."

"I've got access."

"Cool, aye. I know. You still see the old team?"

Johnny's shoulders unhunched and his brow unfurrowed. His split knuckles popped in rhythmic evolutions and he re-took his seat.

"Aye. Squareheid now and again. MacLean is too fucked.
Same with Mikey and that. Useless cunts.
Anyway, you seem to be doing fine.
Still dossing about in bands?"

"Aye, well….kinda. Knocked the music on the head."

"Recruitment drive of '88, eh?"

"Aye."

"Fucking lucky cunt, eh?"

Johnny drew his eyes from Eadie in an act of dismissal. They were so tiny that from a distance he looked like he was wearing a large blank mask with only a nose and mouth crudely etched across the surface.

"You look like shit for such a spivvy cunt."

"I don't sleep much."

Eadie cursed his own meekness. Johnny stood up, went to the counter and threw down a five-pound note. He shouldered his way past Eadie. There was a tremendous urge to relink with this aspect of his old existence. It felt significant. Johnny was the next step

"I've got my great-grandpa's diary."

"What?"

"His diary. He's talking about your papa Dean."

"What about my papa?"

"It's at my flat. I can show you. Might be useful."

***

At the flat, Eadie put on some smooth jazz but quickly remembered himself and switched it off before Johnny had a chance to condemn him. Johnny scouted the place as if he were looking for a hidden object.

"You got any gear?"

"Nah, man. I'm off it."

He felt stupid and pathetic saying something like this. Johnny grinned as if he only half-believed it.

"Where's my great papa's diary then?"

"It's actually my great-grandpa's diary, but Dean makes an appearance in the second entry."

Eadie produced the diary from its place atop his Huxley 3-seater Chesterfield. Johnny snatched it from him and dumped himself on the tan antique leather. He roughly fingered the pages, read a few lines through braided brows.

"How much?"

"Eh?"

"For the book. How much, dafty?"

Eadie looked at Johnny, begged him with his gaze not to become violent. But Johnny was possessed, obsessive-eyed.

"Name the price, cunt."

"I'm not selling it. sorry."

"Naw?"

"No, it's a relic of my legacy."

"Oh, is it?"

Johnny brought out a small blade and brought it to the prominence of Eadie's throat.

"You think because you got lucky enough to get scooped up in some randomised government clean-up operation that you're better than me? Better than your old gran as well, I bet?"

"What, no!"

– Eadie gulped and felt the cold blade nick the hard cartilage of his Adam's Apple, ready to be peeled raw.

"Well, listen. I know what's going on with you. I can see it in your eyes. You can leave the scheme but it never leave you. Try to run away from it, cunt, but it'll catch up to you. It'll fucking catch you and when it does it'll drag you back to the shadows where you belong. You can run away from your gran but she'll find a way of getting you back."

Johnny lowered the blade, released Eadie, and pushed him away. Eadie couldn't talk. He too felt neutered of his old instincts. Violence no longer came easily to him. He had been corporatised. Johnny put the journal in the back pocket of his Kappa popper joggers.

"I'm taking this."

"I can't let you take that."

"Oh? And why is that, cunt?"

"Because it's mine. I know you'll find this hard to believe but I'm going through a trauma greater than anything you've gone through."

Eadie's gut lurched as Johnny lurched forward. He was sick of visitors, from the past or the future.

"Oh, hahaha, really? Is that so?"

Johnny looked flabbergasted by the gaul. Eadie tried to appeal to his long-buried sense of decency.

"Listen, I know you've been through utter shite, but there are no monsters involved in your sadness."

"That's what you think, cunt."

PART
TWO

Don't make me go back there, please. I can't go back. I wouldn't…I couldn't fit back in on the streets. I mean, look at me. I barely fit in here with the programmers and partitioned cubicles, but at least the people around me are polite enough not to draw attention to it. And some of them came in during the recruitment drive so we look out for each other. I can keep working on my corporate mask. Improve my 'core competencies'. I'll eventually master it. I'll keep doing the long hours, get a business account on social media, eat shit and smile at the cunt who's using me as a human toilet. I'll tell myself I'm finally happy. It's not that place. I'm no longer that person. I'm grateful. I'm happy. I should be fucking happy…

Eadie sat in his car which had the radio gutted out and looked up at the windowless Pure-fake building. The Modest Futures Foundation plaque glimmered in the dim-light. The structure was a phallic monolith. Another leviathan. It exacted similar wounds to the skyline, but the way it ate people didn't feel merciful or righteous. This corporate concrete monster scared Eadie because he respected it so much. The sheer potential of the thing gave him vertigo. He barely remembered what life was like before he got the job.

Eadie's job-title was 'Pure Talent' which was equivocal to a grunt by any other workplace parlance. Johnny had taken the diary and now he was back to square one. Facing work seemed harder than ever. Eadie tightened the tender stubs of his nail-bald fingers around the steering wheel. Two teeth fell out that morning. He'd lost all feeling in his pinkie toe, as if the useless appendage was ready to self-sever in an act of gangrene-suicide [6] .

---

6 *Eadie remembered booting a half-deflated football up and down the streets. It was an empty act. And anyway, no one had any skill anymore. That kind of effort probably died when the passion was drained from these pastimes. Football had once been a uniter of the people now it had been separated from meaning. It was once defensible and easy to love. Pure community lifeblood — important! It provided an opportunity for folk to roar at each other and express their suppressed brotherly desires in an acceptable, socially conventional manner. But then football teams didn't exist anymore and hadn't existed for a long, long time. So how could there be passion or a safe manifestation of man's inner territoriality when you were just one wee boy kicking a leather clod through the middens of hell? The memory seemed so empty.*

People with medieval notions of expression thought what he did was disgusting. Immoral. When Eadie told someone where he worked they treated him like a fascist or shill intent on toiletising art or something. Purefakes and their Talents were much maligned in the mainstream media, despite the company supplying tungsten puppet people to the newspaper and television outlets who criticised them. It's not that he could disagree with their assessment, that he was a shill – what he did was a disgusting, immoral, sell-out way to make a living– but those people couldn't see the bigger picture. Eadie destroyed lives, sure, but he also created entertainment. This wasn't expression or art. This was a world of on-site parking, company pensions, cost-effective strategisation, sustainability. Upskilling. Negotiable salaries. Private medical insurance. He didn't really know much about expression or art anymore. It was a numbers game, the satisfactory improvement of key performance metrics.

***

In the office kitchen, he spoke to a drone called Gary who also worked within the concrete beast. Eadie and Gary were scooped up in the drive of '88 but they shared no common association beyond that.

Gary spoke to the air around Eadie but never directly to him. He looked at the plasters on Eadie's fingertips. He raised a long finger to Eadie's mouth.

"You been in a fight, love?"

Eadie could only smile crookedly and embarrassedly.

"Eh? Haha!"

Eadie turned away to put milk in his coffee.

"McInnes is off today."

He winked for some reason.

"His granny died so at least you'll get some peace from the wee
nostril-whistler, eh? Ahaha!"

McInnes's workstation was empty. He couldn't have cared less. Gary imposed his new
gym-tightened physical superiority over Eadie in a single sweeping motion, sending his
rough hands over Eadie's shoulders and straightening his tie for him. Gary touched
three spidery fingers to the nape of Eadie's neck, gently forcing his head forward to
the puckering O of Gary's mouth. He whispered something about filling in a spreadsheet for the last unit. Eadie had to fill out his spreadsheets. Having designed the puppets and filled out a colour-coded prep-form, Eadie had neglected to input the figures into the department database. This was a catastrophic oversight for Talent. Gary
masked his anger with laddish overfriendliness. He asked about the football, did he
go, did he watch it, what about that keeper, eh? He asked him if he was shagging
anyone these days, how he was doing, was he well? This was Gary's way of telling
Eadie that if he didn't do the spreadsheet before his registration, he'd be up the creek.

Gary worked his way up from API integrations, and he could design puppets that almost
had a functioning mind of their own. But not quite, obviously. People in the lower ranks of
the corporation, usually those scraped in during the recruitment drive, thought Gary possessed dark powers. It was hard to disagree. His eyes were black. His algorithms, legendary.

"We're bottlenecking because of that spreadsheet, mm-k, bud?
Head down, bums up."

There was no ghost of a former life in Gary's eyes. Eadie remembered him as a quiet wee stone-kicker emo from two streets away.

At his workstation, the items on his desk seemed to molest him. A stapler, a sharpener. A stack of bot designs. He turned on the computer and logged in. He opened the registration programme. He opened his e-mails to find a bulging inbox of weekend-delivered correspondences, most marked 'urgent'. He had to fill out three corporate questionnaires.

Eadie brought up the Purefake programme, clicked on his dashboard. A tungsten face waited on the monitor. Underneath even the most beloved, cuddly CGI-rendered character a monstrous netted form lay dormant. Pulled wires over a humanoid face. Like a cusk fish, Eadie supposed, which roamed the subterraneous hadal zones with its blunt head. His job was to make them more palatable. To make them look humanoid so people weren't afraid of the way the puppets really looked.

Eadie took off his shoes and socks in the staff toilet and saw his pinkie toe had gone. He pulled out the small flesh-ensconced bone, held it in his plastered fingers. There was no blood. No rough separation line. Just a clean departure. He remembered he had to phone his grandmother that night.

***

Johnny was safely back in the schemesphere of barking dogs and distant screams. He pulled the ring-pull on a can of super lager and supped at the sudsy top-cylinder. The journal sat on his coffee table and there was a glow about it. Johnny knew that he had a part to play in something big. Some of the unanswered questions surrounding his Papa Dean lay within – what happened to him? Why did he kill himself? Why did he abandon his son Bryan and set the Burnie curse in motion. Johnny picked up the book and opened it at a dog-eared page, his heart throbbing in the barred enclosure of his chest.

D could not read but he could see every story that had ever been told like an endless roll of typepaper and so had no requisite for literacy. D warned me against passing through this scheme' a place where itinerant strangers were shot full of holes and middens overflowed as tentacled monsters. He said that we would all populate and pollute the scheme with our broken children. I made the memorandum towards the back of this notebook. Despite being unable to read' D would offer other useful shreds of information. For example:

Did you know that the modern amnesiology is apt to be a general occultist? He may be also an astrologer or a magnetist or a theosophist. But he is foremost an ardent enthusiast for exclusive and unusual lore' not the common and superficial possessions of misguided democratic science. He goes through the forms of study' remains superior to the baser practical ends of life' and finds his reward in the selfsatisfaction of exclusive wisdom.

After a night with D my liminal skin began to itch. Not because his company was arduous but because there was some cellular need within me to hop freightcars. My life before chiptossing for Dean III was of violence. The military had me' you see' and the dreams of that former life are what fuel my running.

Johnny didn't realise it at the time but he had crushed his beer can and the volcanic emission of foam was now bleeding over his clenched fist. He lapped at the excess foam, read on.

we sat at the fire' and I knew this would be my last evening lodging with D. This will also be my last entry for a while. D's voice was an occult instrument as he spoke of his love of magic. I did not ask him to demonstrate his bedevilment but as a liminal I bore him no judgment. You' the reader' may have dismissed me out of hand for my lifestyle but' as I say' I am no eggsucker. I will not judge him for his wants. This is what I came out into the wilderness to see. This man had nothing' and gave me half of it' and we both had abundance.

Johnny was sitting now, a hard lump in his throat, recalling the days when he, Eadie, and the boys would terrorise the community. It felt like an age ago, but it was still his life. He was still that person. If Eadie had been through numerous reincarnations, Johnny was starting to feel like a new spirit, albeit one brimming with sadness.

D explained that butterflies were once human beings. That we had lost our wings in some spiritual conflict. He told me that the butterfly couldn't remember a single thing about being human. When the butterfly awakens in a human body it is filled with a new sorrow and a void where it's wings once fluttered. D said we were all butterflies once' that we could be butterflies again. But we had to stir something within the belly to spark the process. 'Like what?' I asked. He said' 'Remove the things that root you.'
I was profoundly disturbed by this as i'd never once given notion to suicide or murder. But there was something in his eyes. A knowledge and a promise of something newborn. A reason to stop running. start flying. Finally.

I admit' my friend' I did find that intriguing.

Johnny closed over the diary and considered this journal entry. He had never had a family himself, not after a childhood plagued by the brutal fuck-ups he'd descended from. Even Johnny wasn't irresponsible enough to bring another life into this cesspit, to be raised by a selfish and capricious person like himself. Family wasn't for him. He took a moment to feel a quiet gnawing in his chest. Something was moving inside him. Before he knew what was happening, tears filled his eyes and he sobbed uncontrollably, collapsing on the floor of his living room. The pages of the diary were sodden with fallen tears. Johnny had pushed down a barrier. A moment of clarity. He also wanted to be happy and free. Maybe he didn't deserve family, but he deserved happiness.

He had a sudden urge to help Eadie. A sudden longing stirred a churning broth of new compassion. Butterflies couldn't remember a thing in their short two-week lifespan. He longed for that.

***

"Gran?"

HELLO? EADIE, SON, IS THAT YOU?

"Aye."

"HOW WAS YOUR DAY, SON?"

"Fine, aye."

"STILL ENJOYING THE BIG FANCY JOB?"

"It's fine. sorry I haven't phoned in so long."

DON T BE DAFT. YOU RE BUSY MAKING MONEY AND A NAME FOR YOURSELF. YOU RE A NEW MAN AND I LOVE YOU FOR IT. YOUR AULD GRANNY IS ABSOLUTELY FINE. SAME AS I ALWAYS HAVE BEEN. PROUD AS PUNCH.

"Gran...?"

"SON ?"

"I need to ask you something and I want you to be totally honest with me, because I feel like we're never honest with each other. We've never really been that honest with one another."

"WHAT DO YOU MEAN?"

"What happened to your dad? Great-grandpa Boab?"

"Gran...?"

"WE DON T REALLY TALK ABOUT THAT STUFF, SON.
WE CAN T TALK ABOUT THE,
THE *CURSE* OVER THE PHONE."

"Aye, I know. But I would like us to be honest.
I was just wondering why he did it?
I never felt like I could ask before."

"ARE YOU ANNOYED AT ME, SON?"

"What? Of course not."

"YOUR INSTINCTS ARE RIGHT ON THIS.
I REALLY CAN T TALK ABOUT IT."

"I went to see an amnesiologist."

"DAVIE?"

"Aye. He gave me Boab's old journal."

"You'll have to kill me first, cunt."

The phone line went dead.

"Gran?"

***

One time, Eadie had destroyed himself. Erased every cell, every memory, and rematerialized as a new man. The physical body remained the same. It simply destroyed a facet of who he once was – the doss-cunt. He looked in the mirror and saw he was still a reflection of that music-obsessed thug who was so full of life and suffering. Simple human aspic. He knew in the back of his mind that the spiritual body was finally having its say, breaking down the hard keratin proteins in his fingernails and eviscerating the enamel in his teeth until it had reshaped his biological clay into the next vessel. He had no idea what new form his body would take, but it would be purer somehow. This final incarnation would fill him with a deeper, physical happiness. Eadie was almost there. He could see the 'Islands of respite' his great-grandpa talked about. Then he had an awful thought: what if his corporate life was the island of respite? If that was the case then he was wishing away the only happy moment in his life.

***

Back at his apartment, Eadie saw the door ajar. There was a boot pattern on the wood, cracking a vein up the weather-stripping. He edged past the threshold, peering round the hallway wall. A figure was sat on his sofa. Eadie's mouth was cotton-dry as he stared at the back of the intruder's skull. Eadie walked around the couch. It was Johnny, looking like a melancholic, lost child. His great-grandpa's journal rested in his lap. Eadie stared at the back of Johnny's tiny head. Johnny acknowledged his presence without turning to face him.

"I think I'm involved in this somehow."

"Aye, I think you're right."

The journal was now covered in grease and beer sweat.

"What can I do? I…"

Johnny audibly choked on his tears. He gulped down hard and apologised for being so exposed. Eadie couldn't quite believe the transformation in Johnny's attitude, to the point where he doubted the sincerity of his performance. But he went along with it anyway, compelled.

Eadie knew then that this was real. The breakthrough was sincere. His own emotions began to rise.

Johnny was right, Eadie decided. There was something in his face that showed an element of trust

Eadie dug around in his jacket pocket and produced his orphaned pinkie toe. He held up his fingers, void of their nail plates. To complete the illustration Eadie smiled, revealing numerous intervals in his dentition. Johnny didn't look surprised but gulped back another round of tears.

"You can keep watch. This thing visits me every night.
Tries to talk to me. Inflicts these horrible visions. I'm sure it's set this
whole decay in motion. Maybe you can get a look at the thing. Talk to it."

"You not able to talk to it yourself?""

"Only with my mouth closed and my eyes shut.
Even then I'm too paralysed with fear to ask anything useful.
I sort of just let it do its thing and wake up in a sea of my own piss."

"Fine. But whatever is happening to you. I want in on it.
The darkness can have me for its dinner as well.
I'm sick of this place. I want what's next. I'm ready for what's
next. I know a few other people who would want to help you.""

***

That night, Johnny, Squareheid, Mikey, and MacLean showed up at Eadie's door. Once they passed the threshold, they experienced a collective epiphanic moment of clarity. An almighty force sucked their consciousness up into the ceiling area of the flat and their bodies were suddenly empty avatars, docile flesh tanks being observed by a collection of evicted spirits. The men finally saw themselves as others perceived them. They sat huddled under a blanket in the bougie apartment and their ghosts hovered and swirled somewhere in the ceiling.

In his own mind, Johnny had been svelte and wiry, a typical little hard cunt. But now, a doughy-round-the-middle, featureless little man in an ugly, windowless cell revealed itself.

Mikey saw his narrow shoulders bundled beneath a huge, blousy hooded top. A long, bald head emerged from the neckline, ugly irregular fingers from the cuffs. A human insect. He assumed the number of women he'd slept with during his life reflected some truth about his own handsomeness: it was many. Now he considered his history of lovers and realised they were all rape victims. The shame of his predatory instincts descended into his stomach and liquefied in the acid of the worst parts of his nature.

Squareheid had the skull of a macrocephalic cow, his hair a sweat-slicked smear of dirt spread across the sleeping half-moon of his forehead. Bigger than Johnny and Mikey, hypertrophic scarring crossed his neck and forearms. There was the crest of a razor blade across his jaw. He was bigger than most people. The shame of his size struck him. It's tragic simplicity. His clumsy hugeness. The unprovoked bullying and damage he'd perpetrated throughout his lumbering existence added spice to the taste of his shame and this made it all the more gratifying when he felt that part of him die in a dull ache across his groin area.

MacLean was a father to six children he rarely saw. The week before, he walked past his oldest son in the street and didn't even acknowledge his presence. He was an overly relaxed man without repentance having buried any notion of guilt beneath a shallow grave of narcotics. MacLean had cheated, lied, murdered, raped, and gambled his entire selfish life, and it burned like Sirius in his pink chamber. The weight of his vice suddenly brought him to tears under the blanket. He had an urge to reach out to all those he had wronged and declare his changed ways. He quickly realised this, too, would be the superficial folly of a narcissist. Instead, he vowed inside himself never to speak another hideous word again.

The four men lay together in a fractured jigsaw, staring at the ceiling pattern. The swirls of plasterboard spoke secrets of some long-silent universe. And they all went through this enlightenment process together without having to say a word. Their fingers interlinked under the blanket, emptying themselves of a decades-worth of repressed guilt and fear. Outside the window the firmament was set in calming cyan and only delicate contrails breached the canvas. Through a swamp of tears, Johnny choked out the first plea for forgiveness.

"I'm such a fat, horrible cunt."

Mikey squeezed Johnny's fist in his own in a gesture of comfort. He spoke to the god-like energy in the room.

"MATE, I'M A RAPIST. I'VE NEVER TREATED A WOMAN WITH ANY FUCKING RESPECT. I'VE THREATENED THEM WITH DEATH IF THEY REFUSED ABORTIONS. I'VE NEVER HAD RESPECT FOR ANOTHER LIFE. EVER. IN MY LIFE, CHRIST."

Squareheid let his huge head roll onto Mikey's shoulder. He lifted his head and kissed Mikey's chin with a newly acquired tender sympathy.

"i've been a bully my whole life. throwing my weight about, battering folk smaller than me. jesus...i've led a life of utter selfish thuggery."

MacLean was reflectively staring into space but had been clutching Squareheid's knee for the entire out-of-body experience.

"ive got 6 fatherless weans ive been more interested in jagging smack than being a parent. im the worst of the lot."

This was the most profound and human encounter they'd ever shared and their souls met for the first time in 40 years of friendship. Never had they felt so distant from themselves, yet so close to each other. Having exhausted themselves of their ugliest sins, the men started drifting into a warm slumber.

Then there was a noise – footsteps. Johnny shot up and bore full witness to the intruder. A tall figure loomed over Eadie, writhing switchblade claws over his squirming, supine form. Eadie seemed to be in the midst of a sleep terror beneath the towering shadow. Johnny nudged awake his friends, and they made a harmony of silent gasps. They watched transfixed as the intruder caressed the air around Eadie without ever touching his body. Johnny couldn't move and the freedom introduced by the godlike energy had soured into something else, something oppressive. Johnny saw that his friends were also locked in a similar state, unable to move and frozen in a gape of absolute cellular horror. Then the intruder laid its hands upon Eadie's chest and began pulling away long strips of flesh like sweating wallpaper from drywall. Johnny made desperate eye contact with Eadie, who had awoken and was evidently also paralysed. Eadie was petrified but Johnny observed a note of relief in his friend – someone else had finally laid eyes upon the visitor. His mouth was agape in total agonized fright and Johnny saw that Eadie only had 3 teeth left along his top gumline. There was a faint, whispered directive that was inaudible but somehow understood. A babel of voices from the beyond. Johnny was reminded of the familiar prattling patter of a broken junky brain kicked loose of its moorings. Finally, the visitor disappeared into the corner of the room into a mantle of shadow. The smell of urine was overpowering – an acrid, beer-infused stench. Johnny felt a shrill twinge in the root nerve of their pubis and knew the next step would demand a strength that even he was unfamiliar with. He wondered if his friends felt it too until a collective shudder answered that question for him. The presence challenged his sense of strength and mocked his recent vulnerability. Johnny started to think this was all part of some grand cosmic punishment for his past transgressions and he had never known a fear like it. Johnny swooned into a dark stupor and when the light returned Eadie was standing in front of him, naked and limply swaying like a heroin addict with a severe case of the nods. His four remaining toes (two on each side) were hanging on by a thread of tissue, his left-hand fingers had been completely excised rendering his fist a useless ball of bone. Bood raked down his chest.

The visitor had amputated the fingers cleanly but had made a meal of the penis. Eadie begged the men to help him, to give him the emotional fortitude required to fully exonerate himself of the mutilated organ once and for all. The loose flesh had cocooned into a sad, lop-sided trunk. Eadie observed the tumorous, half-torn organ dangling between his legs with some consternation. This was a miserable object – and it was just an object to Eadie now [7]. He felt no connection to it. No affinity, affection, or familiarity. People fought to have the penis uncensored, but Eadie, though progressive, aggrieved the aesthetic ugliness which had caused so much offense to histories suppressors.

Cross-legged on the bathroom floor, he gazed at the penis sunk in its valley. Shallow grooves disappeared into concentrated shadow. Eadie plucked some of the dermis around his testicles roughly, tugging at the strained internal root with his one good hand. The bladder shuddered. His lower abdomen activated. The young team stood still at the doorway of the bathroom and watched.

"We're here for ye, man."

Johnny said reassuringly and tried his best not to wince. Squareheid leaned past the threshold and pulled a pair of nostril scissors out of the cabinet.

"this'll probably do it. it's almost completely off anyway."

---

7 *A Japanese artist called Mao Sugiyama had his penis surgically removed, cooked, and served to paying guests at a public banquet. People with Skoptic Syndrome have also been known to have their nipples removed and clitorises sewn over, so this was far from an undocumented, abnormal inclination. He imagined himself inducted as an honorary to the annuls of transcendent artists.*

He looked at them and passed them to the seated man. Without much consideration at all, Eadie took the scissors, separated the blades and cut down hard on the remaining corpus, neutering himself like a dog. A spray of arterial fluid created a red bouquet against the sterile linoleum. After a series of jagged cuts, he eventually separated the entire penis. Pain set in shortly after, but the shock was enough to keep Eadie from passing out. He drew back the scissors again and made the final incision. He was free. Blackness rushed at him and he was unconscious on the bathroom floor.

"Big steps.
Bounding
steps."

"I know. But it only feels like a bigger deal because I've been conditioned to feel like this organ is the ultimate satellite to channel my desires."

"It'll feel strange
in the final days.
You still have
a few steps before
you can become as free
as a butterfly."

"Suicide?"

"That's the final
step."

"What's before it?"

"Destroying the damaging lie
that has eroded your inner light."

"What…?"

"Quit Purefake.
Decimate your ties
with that world.
Sell your house.
Destroy all connections with peers.
Take to the streets
and live there until
you can arrange the penultimate sacrifice."

"The penultimate sacrifice?"

"This might be the hardest part.
It will require the most
strength
and will hurt more than
your self-castration."

"Why? I don't want to hurt anyone? "

"You won't be.
You'll be doing them
a favour."

"I won't hurt anyone. That part of me is long dead."

"You think you didn't
hurt
people in the corporate world?
Destroying livelihoods.
Sending people back
to the schemes,
people who aren't
strong
enough to survive there?"

"What do I need to do? I don't want to physically harm anyone.
Why would that be necessary?"

"You have no idea,
do you?
That there are things that connect
you to this plane and this body,
beyond
the demands and expectations
of your new vocation?"

"something from my old life?"

"Yes.
You don't have to
do the killing yourself
but you do have to arrange it.
Witness it.
Avoid succumbing to the weaknesses
you've adopted from the
corporate anathema.
Those feelings betray
the true you."

***

Mikey casts the first stone. It strikes Eadie's gran dreadfully hard on the nose, breaking the long bridge of bone flat over the crinkled map of her cheeks. A second rock from Squareheid thumps against her temple leaving behind a purple bloom. MacLean hurls a third. A fourth, a fifth. The brittle structure of the old woman's face caves in on itself. Eadie looks at his feet and tries not to cry. You aren't allowed to cry. She's been cannibalised by the third attack of her cancer, and she probably would've only lived another two years, tops. The strip of tape binding her top half to the tree trunk snaps loose amid the hail of rocks. She falls forward and the film of wet tissue which once wrapped her face detaches, weeping slowly to the brambles below. Dead. A shocking red skull stares back, oozing teardrops of viscera; Eadie marvels at her forgotten face of youth, bandaged in sinew, revealed to him from beneath her aged flesh. As if this young blood mask was a secret she kept from even herself. The cusk fish – eyeless, faceless. A body so inert it's almost inconceivable that it once held the playful soul of his favourite grandparent, the woman who'd raised him.

The cusk fish. Eyeless, faceless. A body so inert it's inconceivable it once held the playful soul of his favourite grandparent.

Aye…

The woman who'd raised him. The woman who called him a 'cunt' and who infected him with guilt and obligation.

The sadness faded quickly. A dense semantic ecosphere filled up Eadie's language centre, replacing the endless reels of course slang and corporate double-speak that had cluttered his neural pathways for the longest time. He suddenly understood. He had been granted the greatest gift of all – articulation. It made sudden sense of his feelings, unmuddied his perception of the objective. He felt a great desire to pull free a book from his paltry, purely decorative bookshelf and consume the knowledge within. He wasn't able to do that before. Eadie looked up at his friends – Johnny, Mikey, Squareheid, MacLean – and the weight of their gesture filled him with profound gratitude. A thought, *had McInnes also killed his own grandmother?*

I know what you're thinking, but the minute I knew she was finally dead I had an **epiphanic** [8] *moment of clarity. A new vocabulary. I was a selfish and* **capricious** [9] *cunt. And so was my grandmother. I was free of the* **manacles** [10] *of our relationship. I can already feel my body changing. Something is moving about inside of me. My accent is starting to leave me…*

---

8 Eadie had never used the word 'epiphanic' before the transformation.

9 Eadie had never used the word 'capricious' before the transformation.

10 Eadie had certainly never used the word 'manacles' before the transformation.

He knew that this was the start of the great metamorphosis.
The carbon rebirth cycle.
It would be painful and unforgettable.
An effortless trauma of imago agony.
To shed the exo-flesh and prepare for nymphal form,
ready to forget all connection with the collective blancmange —
it was something to look forward to.
Total liberation.

***

Squareheid dropped the last rock and it struck the bed of autumn leaves. A silence widened in the wake of its impact. His face was ashen white. Eadie's grandma was gone. Her body as passive as a stone. The red skull stared out at the sky, bloody tears streaming from contracting optic nerves.

Squareheid eventually broke.

"we've killed an auld woman?"

""Aye""

- Johnny's voice held a tone of respect for the dead more than remorse for his actions.

"that didnae…feel right."

Johnny let out a deep sigh.

""I don't think it was meant to, mate.""

Mikey dragged his forearm across his septum and snorted.

"I DON'T KNOW IF I'VE EVER BEEN HAPPY, YOU KNOW THAT?"

Johnny stared at the human blood bag before him.

""I think its better to imagine being alive as a mountain of shit, you know. Everything is terrible. Everything wants to hurt you. Everything fucking hates ye. The world is a shitscape.
So," - he glanced at Eadie - "when those wee islands of respite come along you really appreciate them. We can never be happy. But we can rise our heads above the stench for five minutes and see a dove in flight or a sun setting, then we duck our heads back below the atmosphere and take in the familiar smell.""

"That's cheery."

Mikey kicked at a clod of dirt.

"It is cheery. It's as cheery as things can ever get.""

"I DON'T WANT TO DIE, JOHNNY."

"Haven't you been paying attention? Didn't you see that big shadowy cunt in Eadie's living room? Death isn't the end. This is the hellish part. The bit to be endured with only the odd island of respite to take the edge off. Then we shed all this shite and become something amazing.""

"a butterfly?"

– Squareheid said innocently.
Johnny looked at the wasted figure of Eadie and answered–

"Well....aye.""

***

Eadie stood naked and rain-scarred in the woods, the wind howling, as the young team plastered him in the ooze of the land. He'd lost all his teeth now, was as smooth and bald as one of the Purefake tungsten puppets. Like he'd contracted a deadly wasting disease. In a sense he had, but he'd welcomed infection. Johnny looked at him proudly as he spread dirt and swamp water over Eadie's rapidly-deteriorating human form.

"I suppose....."

– Johnny started.

"You suppose...?"

– Eadie lisped, suddenly grinning.

"I suppose I better....thank_you."

"You'll be next. Then squareheid, then McClean, Mikey, and the rest.
You know the process. You know what's coming. The visitor
has already told me he'll be seeing you on the streets tonight."

Eadie felt calm. The quiet hope in Johnny's face filled his chest with a warm purposeful glow. The fullest and most complete he'd ever felt in his life.

"I cannae believe it. I didn't think I'd ever be happy."

"I know, mate. But you can be. You will be."

Eadie placed a scrawny mitt on Johnny's shoulder and squeezed with the limited effort his atrophied muscles could expend. Then there was the deep exhaustion of imminent hibernation. It was coming. He bade farewell to his friends and a song sang in his heart. He hobbled home.

***

Eadie opened his eyes, straining against a curtain of crusted mucus. He felt like he had emerged from a deep cryostasis, a sleep so necessary, so sudden and regenerative, that he couldn't even remember arriving home. Eadie took in his surroundings. The floor was unfamiliar to him - stained mosaic tiles which indicated he was in a kitchen somewhere. A bowl of dogfood lay in front of him wafting up the pungent stench of meat derivative. Fear struck his chest and a nauseous, physical dread overwhelmed him. Where was he? Before him he saw every possible incarnation of his soul. Dog man, plague rat, cockroach, then a brown, wilting citadel of sentient excrement. They were waiting for him. He had seen the truth. The game. The lie.

"Oh god. Oh, god, no. No. No! NO! NOOOOO! PLEA/E GOD NO!"

Back in the scheme, Johnny and the young team huddled on the street-side kerb as the winter wind tore a terrible howl through the air. Their bones froze to a still lattice. Johnny, MacLean, and Mikey all burrowed into Squarheid's big military jacket absorbing his plentiful heat. Johnny was exhausted. He was so tired he couldn't even see the faces of his friends in the vantablack night, only vague contours of buildings. The wind seemed to pick up as sleep teased his weakened limbs. The stone-throwing had left him oddly fatigued. Perhaps the howling wind was Eadie triumphantly crying his final goodbyes, Johnny thought. He smiled, blowing his breath into his cupped hands, then turned stiffly, sensing a presence standing on the streetside next to him. Something tall and ancient looming just out of his peripheral vision. The others hadn't noticed yet, but Johnny met its gaze. He clenched. It was the Visitor, just as Eadie had promised. But had Johnny fallen asleep? His sight went black and a screed of alien hieroglyphs cursored across his field of vision. Johnny was a believer already, so his brain immediately added meaning to each symbol. The folly of words became glaringly obvious. He released from language, filling the speaker and the listener with jewels of glorious light. Magnets clicked together, levitated from a meaningless surface by a superconductor. If he was sleeping he knew he would be smiling. The guilt washed from him and he was excited about the final act. He knew he didn't entirely deserve this divine clemency. His mind skirted his wasteful life, the recruitment drive of '88. It all left his body like a cleansing sneeze. He felt like his vein-tubes were finally filling with the wisdom of his grandad's journal. He thought about Eadie's mutilated cock. His bald nails and amphibian limbs. Eadie's toothless mouth placing itself over his lap, massaging the meat of his own penis. The thought of being unzipped by the visitor brought him within an inch of climax and he could almost feel the cold wind against his skinless body. When Johnny unclenched his eyes he looked at the cowered, frozen men beside him and knew what he had to do. Squareheid turned to him.

"what is it, johnny?
you've got a mad look in your eye, mate..."

THE
END

¡BONUS!
BONUS!
¡BONUS!
BONUS!

ON SYMBIOSIS AND THE WELCOME LIMITATION OF COLLABORATION

CHRIS KELSO
IN CONVERSATION WITH
DENNIS COOPER

It feels strange talking to Dennis Cooper at this phase of my life. With a new-born child and full-time job dictating the direction of my time and energy, I've been feeling a little out of touch with the writers and artists I'd spent the better part of my selfish 30-year existence devouring - and Dennis Cooper's work certainly shaped my 20's. I was an obsessive fan and a wannabe writer desperate for a publishing credit. To call books like *Frisk*, *Closer*, and *The Sluts* spiritually medicinal would be something of an understatement (although I know Dennis would balk at this description of his impact). Now, when my life feels at its most chaotic, re-connecting with such a formative influence feels like an act of self-care. Like I am checking in with the Dalai Lama or my favourite college professor. We scheduled the interview with the intention of discussing the new film project Dennis and his collaborator Zach Farley were working on. Unfortunately, due to unforeseen circumstances Zach was unable to make the meeting. So, Dennis and I talk about *Room Temperature*, *The Has-Beens*, the reincarnation of a 3-episode TV project for ARTE, and the beauty of successful collaboration. Plus, a bunch of life shit...

CK: Who are your cinematic influences?
With Zach, is there a lot of crossovers of aesthetics or tone in terms
of your individual tastes? What is the sweet spot for both of you?
Bresson seems an obvious influence.
Are there any modern filmmakers you appreciate?

DC: I MEAN, WE'RE PRETTY ALIGNED IN OUR TASTE AND IN-
TEREST AND, I MEAN, SURE HE LIKES BRESSON. I MEAN,
OBVIOUSLY BRESSON IS HUGE TO ME, BUT ZACH REALLY LIKES
BRESSON TOO. IT'S PRETTY RARE THAT WE DON'T AGREE ON
THINGS. WE ALMOST ALWAYS, ALMOST AGREE ON FILM. I DO
TEND TO ENJOY TRICKY AND COMPLICATED AND META AND
        STUFF, AND HE'S NOT INTERESTED IN THAT SO MUCH.
HE'S MORE INTERESTED IN THINGS THAT ARE EMOTIONAL AND
SINCERE. SO THAT'S THE ONLY BIT THAT'S DIFFERENT. BUT
I DON'T KNOW. I MEAN, WE BOTH LIKE THIS EXPERIMENTAL
FILMMAKER NAMED JAMES BENNING. WE'RE BOTH VERY, VERY
BIG FANS OF JAMES BENNING. UM, CHANTEL ACKERMAN, I KNOW
HAS BEEN KIND OF IMPORTANT AND, OH, I DUNNO. THERE'S
PROBABLY A BUNCH, BUT WE'RE, YOU KNOW, WE'RE TRYING
        NOT TO EMULATE ANYBODY. SO THAT'S THE GOAL.

CK: I actually watched *Like Cattle Towards Glow* last night.
It's just been made available to rent on Amazon Prime over here. I
watched that last night and there is nothing else like that around. I
can't even think--

DC: YEAH, THAT WAS TOTALLY AN EXPERIMENT. I MEAN,
BECAUSE, YOU KNOW, I
CERTAINLY HAD NEVER MADE A FILM BEFORE. ZACH HAD MADE
SOME VIDEOS, BUT HE'D NEVER, EVER DONE ANYTHING
NARRATIVE. AND SO, WE WE'RE LIKE FOOLING AROUND REALLY.
THAT WAS IT. WE ONLY HAD $40,000, SO IT WAS EXTREMELY,
EXTREMELY KIND OF AN UNDERGROUND THING, YOU KNOW? THE
PEOPLE IN IT ARE ALL THE GUYS THAT WE PICKED UP OFF
THE STREET. WE HAD THIS GUY WHO WENT OUT LIKE LATE AT
NIGHT AND WENT OVER TO PEOPLE, STANDING IN LINE TO GO
INTO DANCE CLUBS AND SAYING STUFF LIKE,
'HEY, DO YOU WANNA BE IN A MOVIE?'

CK: seriously?

DC: WELL, THAT WAS BASICALLY HOW WE GOT EVERYBODY. THE
MOVIE IS IN ENGLISH, BUT A LOT OF THE GUYS IN IT DIDN'T
                SPEAK ENGLISH VERY WELL. SO, THEY NEVER
REALLY UNDERSTOOD WHAT THEY WERE SAYING. WE WERE
TRYING ALL THESE DIFFERENT KINDS OF FUNNY EXPERIMENTS,
BUT I MEAN, I LIKE THE FILM. BUT IT'S JUST, YEAH.
    AFTER HAVING MADE THE SECOND ONE, WHICH IS MORE
PROFESSIONAL, IT FEELS FUNNY THAT WE JUST RAN AROUND
                          AND DID THAT FILM.

CK: Yeah, I think it really works as a nice little isolated piece, but it does feel almost like a pitch for *Permanent Green Light*.
I also love the fact that one of the segments actually really shocked me because I'm never really shocked when I watch stuff anymore.
I almost forgot how shocking the medium could be.
Like the, the second segment in *Like Cattle Towards Glow* with the, the guy doing spoken word in the club...

DC: OH, YEAH, THE ONE IN THE CLUB. YEAH!

CK: And it really was quite astounding. I hate the word 'transgressive', but I'm thinking about things that, that shock me into a more active state, you know – a response, and that was really, really shocking to me.

DC: YEAH. I MEAN, IT'S ALSO, I MEAN, JUST TO MAKE IT EVEN MORE SHOCKING – RICO, WHO PLAYS THE SPOKEN-WORD GUY, IS ACTUALLY A DANCER, BUT HE AGREED TO DO IT. 'CAUSE WE HAD A HARD TIME FINDING SOMEBODY WHO WOULD BE WILLING TO DO IT AND AMAZINGLY HE AGREED TO DO IT. RIGHT BEFORE WE SHOT IT, HE BROKE HIS SHOULDER AND--

CK: Oh, I noticed that---

DC: YEAH. BUT HE DID IT ANYWAY. AND IF YOU PAY
ATTENTION, YOU SEE THAT HE HAS HIS ARM IN A SLING, BUT
IT ISN'T VERY NOTICEABLE. BUT SO HE WAS, YOU KNOW, HE
WAS GENUINELY IN PAIN. MUCH LESS FROM THE SEX THAN FROM
BEING THROWN AROUND ON THE GROUND.

CK: But that's commitment. That is commitment.

DC: YEAH, HE WAS, YEAH, NO, HE REALLY PULLED IT OFF.
AND HE WAS GETTING PAID LIKE NO MONEY TOO---

CK: But it was a daring sort of performance. Like, you know, it takes a
lot of courage to take on something like that, and it was, it was
incredible.

DC: THANK YOU.

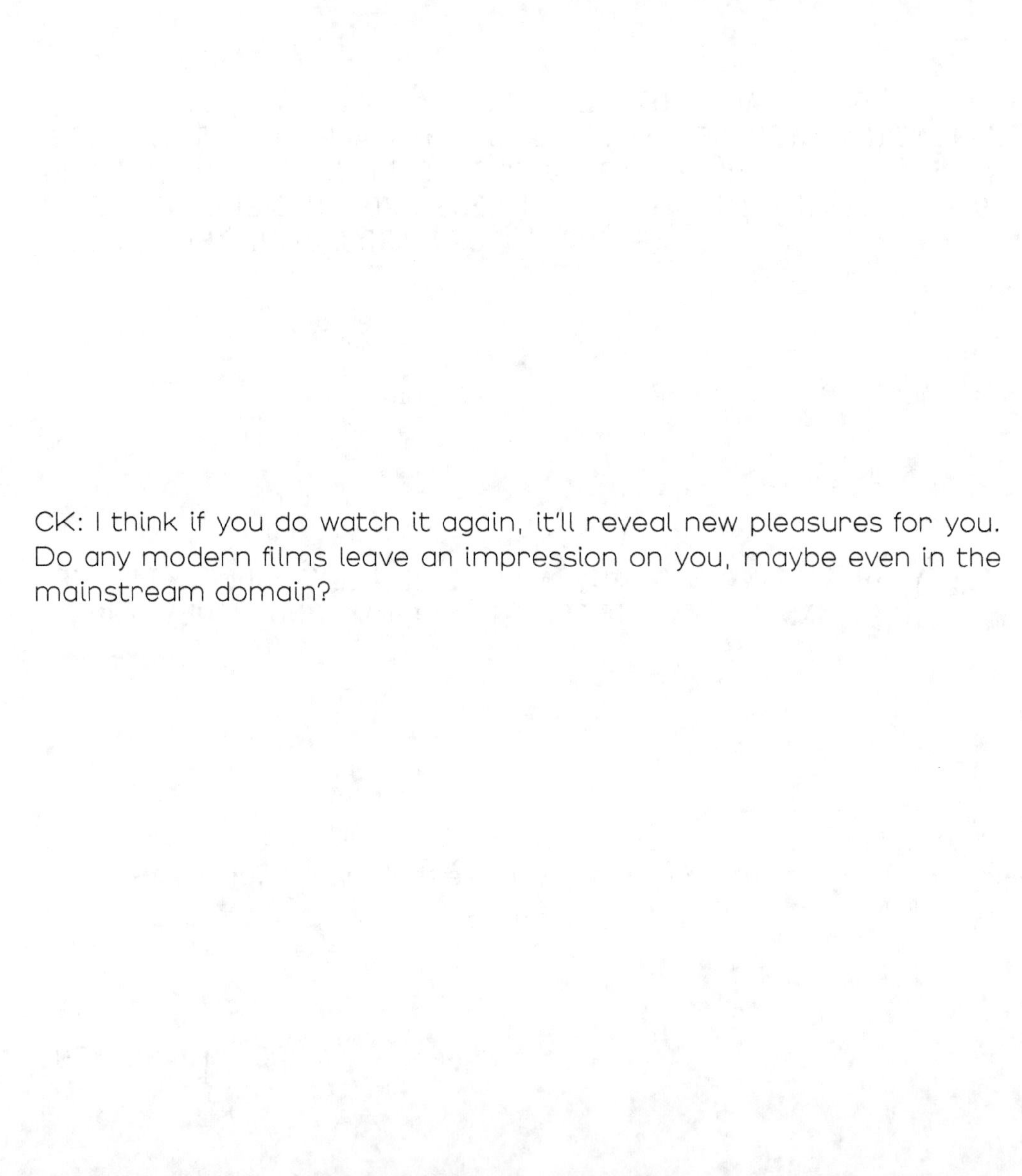

CK: I think if you do watch it again, it'll reveal new pleasures for you. Do any modern films leave an impression on you, maybe even in the mainstream domain?

DC: PROBABLY NOBODY IN THE MAINSTREAM. I MEAN, I LOVE
WES ANDERSON. HE'S A MAINSTREAM, ISN'T HE?

CK: Yeah. Yeah. Oh--

DC: I'M A HUGE FAN OF WES ANDERSON. OH, YOU KNOW, I
LIKE A LOT OF PEOPLE, I DON'T KNOW. I DUNNO IF THEY ARE
INFLUENCES, BUT I MEAN THEY'RE MOSTLY NOT MAINSTREAM.
I LIKE PEDRO COSTA. I MEAN, THEY'RE ALL LIKE WORKING
NOW, BUT THEY'RE NOT REALLY MAINSTREAM. I MEAN, I LIKE
SOME MAINSTREAM FILMS. I LIKE BLOCKBUSTERS CUZ I JUST
LIKE TO ZONE OUT. ALTHOUGH I ONLY WATCH THEM ON PLANES
BECAUSE I'M JUST TRYING TO KILL TIME BECAUSE YOU KNOW,
I GO TO LA AND IT'S LIKE 12 HOURS AND SO I JUST WATCH
THEM TO KILL TIME. BUT I MEAN, I LIKE THAT STUFF. I
MUCH PREFER, LIKE… SHIT. I ACTUALLY PREFER WATCHING
BLOCKBUSTERS OR HORROR MOVIES THAN WATCHING SINCERE
MOVIES, LIKE WHATEVER *CODA* OR--

CK: Do you know something, I've become really worried about my intake recently because, obviously my day job is as a teacher, which is exhausting, and then I've got the new baby – I feel like my art-seeking motivation is diminishing. Like I find myself compelled to watch stuff that keeps me in a relaxed state or helps me escape or something. And, and that's quite concerning because I don't wanna get too comfortable, you know?

DC: OH, THE KID WILL GET A LITTLE OLDER AND YOU'LL GET
                                        YOUR TIME BACK,

CK: I hope so. I hope you're right. Have you both seen the latest
Julia Ducorneau film, *Titane*?

                              DC: I REALLY DIDN'T LIKE *TITANE*.

CK: Oh, you didn't like it. Right. Okay. Oh, interesting. But what is
it about the French who just seem to have this sophisticated palate
when it comes to extreme or outré imagery — did you think
Permanent Green Light would play more successfully in France or
was it just a case of convenience when it came to funding access?

DC: IT WAS, IT WAS. IT WAS MOSTLY JUST THAT WE WERE IN
FRANCE AT THE TIME AND YEAH, IT JUST MADE MORE SENSE.
WE DID THINK IT WOULD BE INTERESTING TO DO A FILM IN
    FRANCE. I MEAN OBVIOUSLY FRENCH FILM IS VERY, VERY
INFLUENTIAL ON BOTH OF US. AS FOR *TITANE*, I MEAN IT
GOT A VERY GOOD RESPONSE HERE, BUT IT GOT A VERY GOOD
RESPONSE EVERYWHERE. PEOPLE IN THE UNITED STATES
                    THOUGHT IT WAS VERY FRENCH. I THOUGHT—

CK: Oh of course, mm-hmm

DC: BUT THEN PEOPLE HERE KEPT SAYING IT WAS VERY AMERICAN. AND I WAS LIKE, WELL, IT COULD ONLY BE BECAUSE OF ME. CAUSE I WAS THE ONLY AMERICAN HAVING ANYTHING TO DO WITH THE FILM. IT DIDN'T SEEM VERY AMERICAN. A COUPLE OF PEOPLE SAID, IT'S LIKE *ELEPHANT* ,AND I'M LIKE, OH IT'S NOTHING LIKE *ELEPHANT*.

CK: No, not at all. No, I don't think so---

DC: I KNOW. NO WAY. BUT THE PEOPLE WHO WERE SAYING THINGS LIKE THAT WERE YOUNG, LIKE, TEENAGERS GIVING ME OPINIONS OR, WELL, THEY WEREN'T REALLY TEENAGERS, BUT WELL, SOME OF THEM WERE--

CK: No, I get, but--

DC: YEAH, MOST OF 'EM WERE IN THEIR TWENTIES, BUT THERE WERE, THERE WAS A 15-YEAR-OLD IN THERE - TWO 15-YEAR-OLDS IN THERE WITH THOSE STRONG REACTIONS TO IT.

CK: I can't even imagine seeing a film like that when I was 15. I know you said you're not a big fan of *Titane*, but if you're 15 it would have a huge impact - especially if you're grow up in scotland and it's a mining town and everything is very repressed and parochial. With *Titane*, you can see it being quite a formative experience for some.

DC: IT'S FUNNY YOU SAY THAT BECAUSE ONE OF THE 15-YEAR-OLDS IS THE GUY, MILO, WHO PLAYED LEON'S FRIEND — THE LITTLE BOY WITH THE LONG HAIR. OH WOW. AND HE WAS JUST A GENIUS. I MEAN ALL OF THE PEOPLE IN THE FILM ARE FANTASTIC AND WERE JUST PERFECT AND EVERYTHING, BUT HE WAS SO SPECIAL. WITH THE OTHER CAST MEMBERS, WE REALLY CAREFULLY CALIBRATED THEIR PERFORMANCES. SO, THEY DID EXACTLY WHAT WE WANTED. BUT WITH MILO, HE WAS SO AMAZING. WE WERE JUST LIKE, DO WHATEVER YOU WANT. YOU KNOW? AND JUST THE OTHER DAY, JUST LIKE LITERALLY THREE DAYS AGO, HE WROTE ME THE SWEETEST THING. BECAUSE HE'S NOW A PROFESSIONAL ACTOR. HE SAYS THAT EXPERIENCE MADE HIM WANT TO BE AN ACTOR. HE WAS WRITING JUST TO SAY HOW MUCH HE, YOU KNOW, HOW MUCH IT MEANT TO HIM TO BE IN THE FILM AND WANTS TO WORK WITH US AGAIN AND STUFF. THIS PERIOD IS OBVIOUSLY VERY FORMATIVE FOR HIM.

CK: That's so cool. I think about writer/director duos, bad example but Christopher Nolan and Jonathan Nolan, Frank and Eleanor Perry, even schrader and scorsese to an extent – how does one inform the other?
Obviously, you both share directing credit but Zach has the credentials and background in visual art and Dennis you're predominantly known as writer, although you do dabble elsewhere.
Is there a process or is the relationship very symbiotic and organic?

DC: YEAH, IT'S REALLY, REALLY SYMBIOTIC, ORGANIC. I MEAN, WE GET ALONG EXTREMELY WELL AND WE'RE VERY DIFFERENT IN A CERTAIN WAY, BUT WE, WE JUST THINK SO MUCH ALIKE. SOMETIMES YOU MEET SOMEONE WHERE YOU JUST SYNC UP. I MEAN, I MET HIM AND WITHIN TWO WEEKS WE WERE COLLABORATING. IT WAS JUST IMMEDIATE. WE IMMEDIATELY STARTED DOING IT BECAUSE IT WAS SO NATURAL. SO YEAH. NO, AND IT'S A GOOD BALANCE BECAUSE I'M PRIMARILY A WRITER AND HE'S PRIMARILY A VISUAL ARTIST AND WHEN WE MAKE THE FILMS THE SCRIPTS ARE MOSTLY MINE AND THE DIRECTION AND THE VISUALS ARE MOSTLY HIM. I MEAN, I LET HIM, CAUSE THAT'S HIS THING, YOU KNOW, I'M NOT A VISUAL PERSON. SO, HE BASICALLY FIGURES OUT HOW TO SHOOT THE FILM. I MEAN WE AGREE ABOUT EVERYTHING AND THEN WE SHOOT IT. HE'S THE DIRECTOR SITTING IN THE DIRECTOR'S CHAIR AND HE'S MAKING ALL THE DECISIONS. COURSE, WE DISCUSS EVERYTHING ALL THE TIME AND I'M MOSTLY WATCHING THE PERFORMANCES AND WORKING WITH THE PERFORMERS. SO, YEAH, IT WORKS OUT REALLY WELL THAT WAY, BECAUSE YOU KNOW, WE KNOW EACH OTHER — OUR STRENGTHS AND WEAKNESSES. YET WE WORK REALLY WELL TOGETHER. IT REALLY FEELS COMPLETELY MUTUAL. IT FEELS LIKE IT'S BOTH OF OUR WORK. IT DOESN'T FEEL LIKE, I MEAN, YOU KNOW, I COLLABORATE WITH A LOT OF PEOPLE. I COLLABORATE WITH JUST THIS DIRECTOR, GISELE VIENE. BUT IT'S HER WORK.

CK: Absolutely.

DC: ZACH AND I, WE SHOOT IT TOGETHER. WE EDIT IT
TOGETHER AND EVERYTHING IS COMPLETELY EQUAL, BUT FOR
SURE HE HAS A REAL STRONG VISUAL SENSE. I WENT TO FILM
CLASSES WHEN I WAS IN COLLEGE BECAUSE I WANTED TO MAKE
                                              FILMS AND
REALIZED VERY QUICKLY WHEN I STARTED TAKING CLASSES
AND TRYING TO MAKE FILMS THAT I WAS JUST, IT WAS JUST
TERRIBLE. I COULD NOT DO IT. IT WAS TERRIBLE. AND I SAW
THE OTHER PEOPLE IN THE CLASS MAKING THESE THINGS AND
I WAS LIKE, 'OH, I CAN'T'. SO, I JUST GAVE UP, BUT I
    ALWAYS WANTED TO MAKE FILMS. IT'S KIND OF PERFECT
BECAUSE YOU KNOW, I TAKE TOTAL OWNERSHIP OF WHAT WE
WERE DOING EVEN THOUGH I'M NOT TECHNICALLY, YOU KNOW,
                    THE 'DIRECTOR', YOU KNOW, SO--

CK: Yeah, but I'm sure Zach would have ideas about the narrative or the way the film should go in terms of individual arcs, etc.
so, I suppose it is *always* kind of mutual. Inter-weaving contributions. I'm sure.

DC: WELL, THERE'S ALSO, YOU KNOW, I MEAN, I DON'T KNOW HOW MUCH YOU WORKED ON THE *STRANGE BIRD* FILM, BUT THE DP HAS A LOT OF INPUT. THAT PERSON IS THE DIRECTOR OF PHOTOGRAPHY. SO, WITH THE FIRST TWO FILMS MICHAEL SALERNO WAS THE DP, AND HE HAD A LOT OF INFLUENCE ON WHAT WAS DONE AND NEXT WE'RE GONNA COLLABORATE WITH THIS FRENCH ARTIST, ACTUALLY SHE'S MAINLY INTO PHOTOGRAPHY. SHE ALSO MAKES FILMS. AND SHE WILL VERY MUCH INFLUENCE WHAT HAPPENS TOO BECAUSE SHE HAS A VERY STRONG VISION. WE LIKE COLLABORATING WITH PEOPLE WHO HAVE A REALLY STRONG VISION. SO, THE DP DOESN'T REALLY GET AS MUCH CREDIT AS THEY SHOULD.

DC: I MEAN, WHEN WE WERE MAKING *PERMANENT GREENLIGHT*, WE HAD SUCH LITTLE TIME, AND WE HAD SUCH AN ELABORATE SHOOT PLANNED OUT, WE HAD TO KEEP CUTTING IT. THERE'S A SCENE WHERE THERE'S A FUNERAL AND ORIGINALLY, WE HAD LIKE 28 SHOTS WE WERE GONNA DO. AND THE GUY WHO WAS COORDINATING THE PRODUCTION WAS JUST LIKE 'NO WAY CAN YOU DO 28 SHOTS, YOU HAVE TWO HOURS' OR WHATEVER. SO, THEN WE COULDN'T FIGURE OUT WHAT TO DO. BUT OUR DP, MICHAEL, WAS JUST LIKE, 'HERE'S WHAT WE DO'. WE DO A TRACKING SHOT AND WE, AND, AND WE CUT IT DOWN. IT WOUND UP BEING FOUR SHOTS AND HE JUST FIGURED IT OUT LIKE THAT. AND I DON'T KNOW WHAT WE WOULD'VE DONE IF HE HADN'T BEEN THERE AND KNOWN HOW TO DO THAT.

CK: I'm glad you brought up Michael, because obviously he's a great publisher with Kiddiepunk. I really like their output. It's obvious he has a very strong visual style that seems to compliment your work so well.

DC: OH, YEAH.

CK: Can you tell me a bit about your next project together, *Room Temperature*?
Will it be a French production? I'm sure I read somewhere that this film was going to be set in LA, but I may have imagined that scrap of information. And is it true you're also both working on a three-episode television series for the ARTE channel, to be directed by your long-time collaborator, Gisèle Vienne?

DC: SURE, WE'RE SHOOTING IT IN SOUTHERN CALIFORNIA. THE
EXECUTIVE PRODUCERS ARE IN MARSEILLE BUT EVERYTHING'S
GOING TO HAPPEN IN LOS ANGELES AND THE CO-PRODUCERS
ARE IN LOS ANGELES. AND THEN WE ALSO HAVE A
CO-PRODUCER BECAUSE THE PEOPLE WHO DID
PERMANENT GREENLIGHT, LOCAL FILMS, ARE GONNA DO THE
POSTPRODUCTION. THEY'RE CO-PRODUCERS SO TECHNICALLY
IT'S MORE OF A EUROPEAN PRODUCTION, BUT WE'RE GONNA BE
WORKING WITH AMERICAN CAST WHEN WE ACTUALLY MAKE THE
FILMS IN LOS ANGELES. I MEAN, WE DO HAVE THE FRENCH
DP. THE ONLY PERSON WE CAST WHO ISN'T AMERICAN IS THIS
YOUNG ACTOR WHO'S GONNA PLAY ONE OF THE PARTS. HE'S
FRENCH AND WE'RE FLYING HIM OVER. BUT OTHERWISE, I
MEAN, IT'S GONNA FEEL TOTALLY AMERICAN.
THERE'S NOTHING ABOUT IT THAT'S GONNA SEEM FRENCH.

CK: Mm, okay. That, that sounds great. I mean, just when you go talking about Gisèle Vienne before, are you and Zach also working on some three-episode television series as well?

DC: OH BOY, WE DID. HORRIBLE.

CK: Oh, sorry.

DC: NO, IT WAS FOR ARTE, DO YOU KNOW ARTE?

CK: Yeah. Oh yeah. The channel. Yeah, yeah, yeah.

DC: BASICALLY, WE WERE DOING A TELEVISION SERIES FOR
ARTE. THAT WAS THE IDEA AND GISÈLE WOULD DIRECT, AND
ZACH AND I WERE WRITING IT AND IT SEEMED GREAT FOR A
WHILE, BUT, UM, THEY JUST KEPT DEMANDING MORE AND MORE
AND MORE AND MORE AND MORE COMPROMISES AND MORE AND
MORE AND MORE REWRITES. AND THIS WENT ON FOR 5 YEARS.
    IT WAS SO MUCH WORK AND WE GOT SO LITTLE MONEY AND
ULTIMATELY IT GOT TO THE POINT WHERE THEY PUSHED US TOO
FAR. AND WE GOT TO THE POINT WHERE IT WAS LIKE, 'WE
CAN'T, WE CAN'T LIVE WITH THIS'. WE'RE NOT GUNS FOR
HIRE. WE HAVE A VISION. WE WANNA MAKE THE THING AND
THEY KEPT SAYING, IT HAS TO BE MORE CONVENTIONAL, MORE
CONVENTIONAL, MORE LIKE 'THIS'. SO ULTIMATELY IT FELL
                         APART, BUT AFTER 5 YEARS.

CK: shit.

DC: SO THAT WAS THAT. AND THEN THE IDEA WAS TO CHANGE
IT INTO A FILM. SO, THEN ZACH AND I REWROTE THE SCRIPT,
AND THE PLAN WAS TO MAKE IT INTO A FILM SCRIPT AND FOR
GISÈLE TO DIRECT. AND THAT MAY OR MAY NOT HAPPEN, I
SUSPECT NOT. THEN I GOT THIS IDEA THAT I WAS GONNA TURN
IT INTO A NOVEL, THAT WE WOULD TURN IT INTO A NOVELLA
                        WITH MINIMAL DIALOGUE CALLED
                                   THE HAS-BEEN.

CK: I was gonna ask about that. I knew you and Zach, that there was talk about you working on that book. And---

DC: YEAH, SO WE WORKED ON THAT FOR A REALLY LONG TIME AND NOW IT'S CHANGED INTO SOMETHING ELSE. NOW IT'S GOING TO BE LIKE A RADIO PLAY, BUT AT THE SAME TIME IT'S A NOVEL.

CK: Okay.

DC: IT'S PROBABLY GONNA BE AVAILABLE AS AN AUDIO BOOK
    OR MAYBE AS A LISTENING EXPERIENCE. BASICALLY, A
NOVELLA THAT'S PERFORMED LIKE IT'S A RADIO PLAY. SO
THAT'S THAT. I THINK THE BEST WAY TO DO IT, BECAUSE I
THINK IT'S PRETTY INTERESTING ON THE PAGE – BUT IT WAS
   REALLY MEANT TO HAVE THESE PERFORMANCES AND VOICES...

(the screen goes green)

DC: OH, I DUNNO WHAT HAPPENED.

CK: Ha-ha, I like it. I think you should keep it. I like it.

DC: YOU LIKE IT? OKAY, COOL. I LOOK LIKE A ROBERT
EGGERS FILM NOW, YOU KNOW. SO YEAH, THAT'S GONNA BE
OUR NEXT PROJECT AFTER WE FINISH THE FILM. WE'RE GONNA
DO THIS RADIO PLAYBOOK NOVEL THING. IT'S ABOUT A WOMAN
WHO'S A VENTRILOQUIST, WHO'S THE DAUGHTER OF SOMEONE
VERY FAMOUS - HE'S LIKE THE MOST FAMOUS PERSON IN THE
WORLD. IT'S BASED ON A TRUE STORY. BECAUSE THERE WAS
THIS GUY WHEN I WAS A KID NAMED EDGAR BERGEN. AND HE
WAS EVERYWHERE. HE WAS. HE WAS LIKE ELVIS. I MEAN YOU
COULDN'T GET AWAY FROM HIM, HE WAS SO FAMOUS, AND HE
    HAD THIS DUMMY NAMED CHARLIE MCCARTHY. VERY, VERY
      FAMOUS AND HE DIED. THEN THERE WAS HIS DAUGHTER
CANDACE BERGER. AND IF YOU KNOW WHO THAT IS, SHE'S LIKE
        AN ACTRESS. SHE WAS IN A LOT OF FILMS IN THE
SEVENTIES AND EIGHTIES. ANYWAY, IT'S KIND OF BASED ON
THAT. BUT ANYWAY, IN OUR VERSION THE DAUGHTER INHERITS
THE PUPPET, WHO SHE HATED BECAUSE THE PUPPET ALWAYS
GOT MORE ATTENTION THAN SHE DID. NOW SHE LIVES WITH
THIS PUPPET, AND SHE BASICALLY TREATS IT LIKE IT'S A
                HUMAN BEING. CHAOS ENSUES.

CK: sounds fucking great. That sounds brilliant. It's--

DC: FUNNY. IT'S GOOD. IT'S GONNA BE GREAT.

CK: Yeah. Yeah. That sounds good. speaking of Gisèle, I adore your previous work together, Dennis. It's nothing new to suggest that you explore taboo themes in a way that's uniquely, and oddly, compassionate.

To me, *Jerk* is a fascinating example of this, fascinating in both its execution and eventual life cycle.

Jerk first appeared as a short story in your *Ugly Man* collection but more recently was staged as a marionette show, directed by Gisèle Vienne (featuring music by Peter Rehberg, with puppetry performed by French ventriloquist Jonathan Capdevielle).

Could you see a cinematic adaptation of *Jerk* in the future, or has the medium of puppetry become key to its genetic material?

DC: IT'S ALREADY A FILM, ACTUALLY.

CK: Oh seriously,

DC: IT'S A FILM. IT JUST GOT RELEASED. IT JUST GOT RELEASED IN FRANCE TWO WEEKS AGO. IT'S A FILM.

CK: Oh my God. sorry, but that is mind blowing. Well---

DC: YEAH,

CK: Just when I think I've got my finger on the pulse of what you're doing!

DC: ACTUALLY, SEVERAL PEOPLE HAVE ASKED IF THERE'S A
SCREENER WITH ENGLISH SUB - IT'S IN FRENCH. SO, IF I
GET HOLD OF ONE, I'LL SEND IT TO YOU BECAUSE A BUNCH OF
PEOPLE HAVE ASKED ME FOR THAT. I'LL SEND YOU THE LINK.
IT'S GOOD. IT TURNED OUT REALLY WELL. YEAH. WE ADAPTED
IT BECAUSE JONATHAN PERFORMED THAT. AS YOU'LL SEE HE
DID IT FOR SUCH A LONG TIME, TOURING THE SHOW AND HE
   FLEW ALL OVER THE WORLD TO DO IT. THEN HE WAS LIKE
'I CAN'T DO THIS ANYMORE'. SO, HE STOPPED. I MEAN, IT
DEPENDS ON HIM SO MUCH THAT WE DECIDED TO JUST MAKE
   THIS FILM. IT'S ACTUALLY REALLY GOOD. IT'S A VERY
INTENSE PIECE. I DON'T KNOW IF YOU'VE HEARD THAT, BUT
   IT'S VERY INTENSE. I MEAN, PEOPLE FAINT AND STUFF.

CK: Wow.

DC: IT'S KIND OF STRANGE HOW THAT WORKED OUT. IT JUST
SORT OF CAME OUT.

CK: That sounds fantastic – and when you were talking about
The Has Been being an audio experience, like I know you've also
branched out into video game territory, a kind of virtual walk-through
of a haunted house that premiered at The Pinault Foundation in Paris.
The project brought together a lot of interesting creative voices, from
curator sabrina Tarasoff to musician Puce Mary.

DC: WELL, THERE'S THAT TOO.

CK: Yeah. And again, there's a lot of collaboration happening with
curators and musicians. so, I've got two questions:
how do you feel about video games?
And the second question you've kinda answered already,
but how important is collaboration to you? Like the process of it?

DC: I LOVE VIDEO GAMES. UM, THEY'VE BEEN A REALLY BIG INFLUENCE ON ME. I WROTE A NOVEL CALLED *GOD JR* THAT MOSTLY REVOLVES AROUND THAT WORLD. I'M LIKE A NINTENDO GUY, SO IT'S MOSTLY NINTENDO. UM, BUT YEAH, NO, I MEAN, IT'S JUST, BECAUSE I DON'T LIKE CONVENTIONAL FICTION, I JUST DON'T AND I'M ALWAYS LOOKING FOR DIFFERENT WAYS TO MAKE THINGS MOVE FORWARD, BUT IN AN UNUSUAL WAY. AND I REALLY GOT OBSESSED WITH HOW IN VIDEO GAMES, YOU KNOW, THAT THERE'S THIS FORWARD MOVEMENT AND YOU HAVE A CERTAIN AMOUNT OF FREEDOM. IT'S VERY SIMPLE WHAT HAPPENS, BUT YOU HAVE TO SOLVE PUZZLES, OR YOU HAVE TO DO THIS AND THIS. SO, I GOT REALLY EXCITED BY THAT IDEA.

CK: Totally.

DC: AND I ALSO REALLY LIKE THE SPACE INSIDE VIDEO GAMES. I THINK IT'S VERY BEAUTIFUL. IT'S VERY IMMERSIVE AND YOU KIND OF BELIEVE IT, BUT IT'S SO FAKE AND EVERYTHING'S KIND OF, YOU KNOW, LIKE KIND OF CUTE, BUT YOU JUST KIND OF GO WITH IT. AND SO YEAH. THEY WERE A BIG INFLUENCE ON ME. I MEAN, YOU KNOW, LIKE *THE MARBLE SWARM* IS PROBABLY REALLY INFLUENCED BY THE VIDEO GAMES AND STUFF TOO. SO, SO YEAH, I REALLY, REALLY LIKE VIDEO GAMES AND AS FOR COLLABORATION WELL...

CK: Yeah...

DC: YEAH. I'VE ALWAYS COLLABORATED. I MEAN I ALWAYS
COLLABORATED. THERE WERE TIMES EARLY ON WHEN I WAS
LIKE IN CHARGE OR SOMETHING. I MEAN, WHEN I WAS A KID,
YOU KNOW, WHEN I WAS A REALLY LITTLE KID. I SET UP A
THEATRE IN OUR ATTIC AND I GOT TOGETHER WITH LIKE MY
SIBLINGS AND PEOPLE FROM THE NEIGHBOURHOOD AND WE PUT
ON SHOWS. WE HAD A THEATRE COMPANY, YOU KNOW, AND PUT
ON PLAYS. SO, I WAS DOING THAT WHEN I WAS LIKE 10, YOU
KNOW? AND THEN I USED TO DO HAUNTED HOUSES IN OUR BASE-
MENT, AND I WAS THE BOSS. BUT YOU KNOW, ALL THE OTHER
PEOPLE COLLABORATED WITH ME. I REALLY, REALLY LIKED IT.
I REALLY LIKED IT A LOT TO THIS DAY. UM, ESPECIALLY BE-
CAUSE YOU KNOW, WITH BEING A WRITER, YOU KNOW THIS VERY
WELL TOO, IT'S LIKE YOU'RE GOD, WHEN YOU'RE A WRITER.
YOU CAN, YOU KNOW, BASICALLY DO WHATEVER YOU WANT. BUT
WHEN YOU'RE COLLABORATING, YOU HAVE TO LISTEN TO WHAT
OTHER PEOPLE ARE SAYING AND THINK ABOUT THEIR WORK OR
CONSIDER THEIR THINGS. AND THE THING ABOUT THE THEATRE
IS REALLY INTERESTING AS A JUMPING OFF POINT FOR ME. IT
ALL STARTED WITH THE THEATRE THING AND NOW IT'S LIKE I
HAVE TO THINK ABOUT WHAT GISÈLE WANTS. AND THEN SO YOU
HAVE TO ADJUST WHAT YOU'RE DOING TO KIND OF FILL THEM
                              IN OR, YOU KNOW WHAT I MEAN?

CK: Mm-hmm.

DC: SO THAT WAS REALLY EXCITING TO ME CONSIDERING I'D
ALWAYS JUST MADE EVERYTHING UP, BUT TO HAVE AN ACTUAL,
THE KIND OF LIKE LIMITATION OF HAVING A PHYSICAL PER-
SON THERE - IT'S, WELL, IT'S A WELCOME LIMITATION AND
IT'S ALSO REALLY EXCITING...

CK: You still enjoy collaborating in the theatre...

DC: I LIKE WORKING WITH THEATRE, BUT THE FILMS ARE GREAT
TOO. I'VE GOTTEN KIND OF SPOILED BECAUSE ZACH AND I ARE
SO LIKEMINDED. I MEAN, I'VE WORKED WITH GISÈLE FOREVER
AND I DON'T HAVE ANY EGO ABOUT THAT KIND OF STUFF. IT'S
REALLY, REALLY EASY FOR ME TO JUST TAKE A BACKSEAT AND
FILL IN WHAT THEY NEED. I DON'T HAVE LIKE ISSUES ABOUT
CONTROL. I DON'T EVEN KNOW ANY CONTROL FREAKS.

CK: That's probably one of the the keys to a successful collaboration, right? There can't be any ego or total control. I feel the same about my own writing, but I also like to professionally collaborate as well. It's very fulfilling. I'll never collaborate with people that I don't admire or respect. so, I'm never forced to collaborate with people. It's not as if it's gonna be two completely diametrically opposed visions colliding. They're going to be kind of similar. And you know, I'm probably a bit more insecure in my ability and vision so I always think that whatever somebody else brings to table is a great idea. You know, and it just enhances it.

DC: JUST THE OTHER DAY I WAS WONDERING, LIKE, HOW YOU COLLABORATED WITH DAVID ON THE CRONENBERG BOOK. LIKE HOW DID THAT WORK? HOW DID YOU GUYS DO THAT?

CK: That was really easy. It was, it was very similar to you and Zach probably. We're very similar. sure, he's a Harvard-educated American with an academic background and I'm a sort of, you know, I'm like an average student from this nowhere place called Cumnock, which was voted the worst place in the UK not that long ago - so on the surface we're these radically different people with different upbringings, but the influences that comprise our artistic personality are almost identical.

DC: OKAY.

CK: Plus, David is no control freak and I'm not controlling. I think as long as nobody is a maniac for control it'll all work out pretty well, do you know what I mean? Then it'll be fine. It was so easy, and then I wrote a story with Brian Evanson recently, and--

DC: YEAH, YEAH, YEAH, YEAH. HOW WAS THAT? YEAH.

CK: Again, just really easy.

DC: YOU SENT THE STORY BACK AND FORTH?

CK: Just, just back and forth. And it was, it was so easy. I've never had a negative collaboration. Have you? You don't have to name names, but have you ever had a negative experience collaborating?

DC: NOT THAT I FOLLOWED THROUGH ON. THERE WAS A GUY WHO ASKED ME TO COLLABORATE WITH HIM AND I WAS SUPER INTERESTED, BUT THEN WHEN WE STARTED WORKING TOGETHER IT DIDN'T PAN OUT. ACTUALLY, I STILL REGRET THIS. IT WAS A LONG TIME AGO. I WAS GONNA WRITE A FILM FOR THIS YOUNG DIRECTOR AND HE WAS DAVID LYNCH'S ASSISTANT. IN FACT, HIS NAME'S ALL OVER DAVID'S WORK, LYNCH'S WORK. AND HE, DAVID LYNCH, GAVE HIM A MILLION DOLLARS TO MAKE A FILM AND HE WANTED TO WORK WITH ME ON THE SCRIPT. AND I WAS REALLY EXCITED BECAUSE, YOU KNOW...

CK: Mm-hmm

DC: THIS GUY WAS COOL, BUT WE COULD NOT AGREE. WE SIMPLY COULD NOT AGREE ON ANYTHING. IT WAS JUST LIKE, HE JUST KEPT WANTING TO DO ALL THIS SHIT AND I DIDN'T WANNA DO WHAT HE WAS GONNA DO. SO ULTIMATELY, I WAS JUST LIKE, 'DUDE, YOU HAVE TO DO THIS YOURSELF. CAUSE I CAN'T. WE DON'T AGREE.' AND IT'S JUST FRUSTRATING TO ME. AND THEN OF COURSE HE NEVER MADE IT ANYWAY. SO IT'S ALL KIND OF SAD, BUT SO YEAH, THERE'S ONE.

CK: I'm curious as to how you felt about Diarmuid Hester's critical analysis of *Wrong*? I've heard that there are a few factual discrepancies and there may be aspects of Diarmuid's interpretation of your work that you feel are overextended — yet *Wrong* is such an undeniably intense labour of love. You strike me as a man of great humility so was it surreal having such a comprehensive and academic retrospective written about you?

DC: IT'S DEFINITELY SURREAL.
OVER TIME I'VE BEEN SORT OF LIKE FIGURING OUT HOW TO
DEAL WITH THAT WHOLE SITUATION. I'M REALLY, REALLY,
REALLY GRATEFUL AND BLOWN AWAY THAT HE DID IT AND HE
DID A LOT OF WORK. HE SAYS A LOT OF GREAT THINGS IN IT
AND, YOU KNOW, I'VE TALKED TO HIM ABOUT IT. IT'S JUST
LIKE, HE HAD A KIND OF IDEA OF HOW TO INTERPRET MY
WORK THAT'S TOTALLY WIDE OF THE MARK. AND I UNDERSTAND
THAT'S WHAT THEY DO. RIGHT. SO, IT'S LIKE, OKAY, I'M
GONNA DO IT THROUGH PUNK OR WHATEVER. I HAVE THIS IDEA
OF MY LIFE AND WHAT INFLUENCED ME AND STUFF THAT'S KIND
OF BIGGER THAN THAT, YOU KNOW? IT'S LIKE, WELL, DUDE,
YOU DIDN'T MENTION THE INFLUENCE OF PSYCHEDELIC MUSIC
IN THE SIXTIES. YOU NEVER MENTIONED LOW-FI INDIE ROCK
OR EARLY TECHNO, WHICH WAS JUST AS IMPORTANT TO ME.
YOU KNOW? I DON'T HAVE A HUGE PROBLEM WITH IT. JUST
WHEN PEOPLE ASK ME, YOU KNOW, SOMETIMES THEY'LL SAY
MY ANARCHISM WAS INFLUENCED BY PAUL GOODMAN. I READ A
PARAGRAPH OF PAUL GOODMAN IN 1970. I DIDN'T LIKE IT.
SO, I'M JUST LIKE, DUDE, THAT JUST DIDN'T HAPPEN. HE
MADE IT SEEM LIKE I'M FRIENDS WITH PATTI SMITH. I'M
NOT FRIENDS WITH PATTI SMITH. I'VE NEVER BEEN FRIENDS
WITH PATTI. SO, I'M LIKE WHERE DID YOU GET THIS? IT'S
LIKE THAT. CAUSE HE CAME HERE AND INTERVIEWED ME, AND
I'D SAY, WELL, 'DON'T YOU WANT TO ASK ME ABOUT THIS'?
AND HE'D BE LIKE, 'WELL, I ALREADY READ THIS STUFF ON-
LINE'. SO, YOU KNOW, THERE ARE LITTLE THINGS, BUT GEN-
ERALLY I'M HAPPY WITH THE BOOK AND I'M SUPER GRATEFUL
AND IT'S JUST LITTLE THINGS. PEOPLE LIKE TO PICK AN
ANGLE AND THEN THEY SEE YOUR WORK THROUGH THIS ANGLE.

CK: It's great mythologizing on Diarmuid's part.
so, last question, because I know you're busy as well and, and I can hear
the baby screaming, so--

DC: OH NO!

CK: You're much more than a writer, as evidenced by your work with
Zach. In a way, do you feel like *I Wished* was a concluding statement to,
not just the long-running George Miles Cycle, but also to your writing
of novels in general? Or can we expect a foray into standard genre
fiction? I'd love to see a Dennis Cooper science fiction story...

DC: I DON'T KNOW HOW TO DO IT. I NEVER STUDIED FICTION. I PLAY ON EXPERIMENTAL STUFF, AND I DO ALL THESE OTHER THINGS, BUT I DON'T KNOW HOW TO DO A LOT OF STUFF AND I DON'T WANNA KNOW HOW TO DO. I MEAN, I NEVER LEARNED HOW TO DO THOSE THINGS. I CAN'T DO IT. I DON'T LIKE PLOT. I DON'T LIKE PSYCHOLOGICAL DEVELOPMENT. I DON'T LIKE ALL THAT STUFF, BUT I ALSO DON'T HAVE A FUCKING CLUE HOW TO DO IT. I'VE READ VERY, VERY LITTLE SCIENCE FICTION LITERATURE, LIKE VERY LITTLE, VERY LITTLE. I LIKE GENRE. I USED TO LIKE DETECTIVE NOVELS AND STUFF. I USED TO REALLY LIKE, YOU KNOW, ALL THOSE GUYS, BUT I CAN'T IMAGINE DOING IT. I MEAN, I CAN, MAYBE, BUT IT WOULD BE VERY, VERY DIFFICULT. I THINK I HAD TO STICK TO MY WEIRD SHIT. THE BOOK *I WISHED*, YOU KNOW, IT WASN'T MEANT TO BE PART OF THE CYCLE OR ANYTHING LIKE THAT. IT'S JUST THAT I WANTED TO WRITE A REALLY, RE-ALLY PERSONAL BOOK THAT WAS EMOTIONAL. I'D NEVER DONE THAT BEFORE. I CHOSE GEORGE BECAUSE THAT'S THE MOST DIFFICULT THING FOR ME. AND SO, I DID THAT AND THEN IT'S LIKE, WELL, IF I'M GOING TO DO RIGHT BY GEORGE, I HAVE TO MENTION THE CYCLE BECAUSE I WROTE THE CYCLE FOR HIM. BUT I UNDERSTAND WHY PEOPLE SAY IT IS, BUT I DON'T THINK IT'S PART OF THE CYCLE. I FEEL LIKE IF YOU READ *I WISHED* AND YOU DIDN'T KNOW WHAT THE CYCLE WAS, YOU COULD JUST THINK IT WAS, I JUST MADE IT UP OR
SOMETHING.

CK: I was gonna ask you, do you ever think that, because *I Wished* is such a personal book, people asking you questions about it kind of trivializes the impact or memory of---

DC: NO, NO. WITH A BOOK LIKE THAT, YOU HAVE TO REALLY UNDERSTAND THAT THEY'RE REALLY OUTSIDE YOU AND THEY DON'T KNOW GEORGE. I MEAN, NO ONE HAS OVERSTEPPED THE MARK YET. I HAVEN'T HAD A PROBLEM WITH THAT AT ALL. I HAVE PROBLEMS WITH DIFFERENT KINDS OF THINGS. I HAVE PROBLEMS WHEN PEOPLE WHO READ BOOKS TRY TO OBJECTIFY THE CHARACTERS AND THINK THEY'RE HOT OR SOMETHING. TO ME THAT SEEMS SO DISRESPECTFUL. CAUSE I TRY SO HARD NOT TO MAKE THEM JUST SEXY BOYS, YOU KNOW? I HATE THAT STUFF. SO THAT BOTHERS ME. BUT NO, IT IS WEIRD TO TALK ABOUT THAT BOOK. I KIND OF KNOW HOW TO DEAL WITH IT NOW.

CK: Yeah.

DC: EITHER YOU FEEL IT OR, OR YOU CAN'T RELATE TO IT OR SOMETHING.

CK: Dennis. Listen, thank you so much. Thank you

DC: THANKS, MAN.

CK: Next time you're in Glasgow give me a call.

DC: TOTALLY. AND IF YOU'RE IN PARIS LET'S DEFINITELY
GRAB A COFFEE OR SOMETHING...

CHRIS KELSO HAS BEEN NOMINATED FOR THE BRITISH FANTASY AWARD, THE BRAVE NEW WEIRD AWARD, AND THE PUSHCART PRIZE, AS WELL AS BEING PRAISED BY FORERUNNERS INCLUDING SAMUEL DELANY, RAMSEY CAMPBELL, AND DENNIS COOPER.
HE'S ALSO AN ACCOMPLISHED EDITOR AND ESSAYIST WITH NUMEROUS NON-FICTION TITLES ON ARTISTS WHO EXPLORE SIMILARLY DARK VEINS, AS WELL AS COLLABORATIONS WITH AUTHORS AND ARTISTS RANGING FROM BRIAN EVENSON TO MEMBERS OF SUNN O))).
YOU CAN CHECK OUT HIS WORK AT
WWW.CHRIS-KELSO.COM

THANKS TO ELLE NASH FOR GIVING THE BOOK AN EMPATHETIC EDIT
AND TO EWAN MORRISON FOR CASTING A CRITICAL EYE OVER
THE MSS/CONTRIBUTING TO THE METYMPSYCHOSIS PROJECT. AND THANKS
TO EVAN FEMINO FOR TAKING A CHANCE WITH IT.

THIS BOOK IS DEDICATED
TO MY OLD FRIEND FRASER WHO PASSED AWAY LAST YEAR,
AND TO MY BEAUTIFUL WIFE AND DAUGHTER -
FOR HELPING ME FINALLY TRANSFORM INTO A REAL PERSON.

Edging on Death (aka Bobby Lafollette) produces art focusing on Eroguro, BDSM, kink, fantasy, horror, Grind House, noise, and more with sometimes humorous tongue in cheek spirit. The name Edging on death came about after he found himself banned from virtually every social media outlet for the content of his work, therefore the brand and style has always been "edging on death". All art is hand drawn with pencil and ink then transferred to comics, coloring books, stickers, and whatever else he can create on his own with a printer. Edging on Death provided illustrations for Kelso's previous novella, Voidheads.

FERAL DOVE

PUBLISHED BY FERAL DOVE BOOKS

FIRST EDITION

ISBN 979-8-218-66500-5

THANK YOU FOR BEING HERE.
BOOK DESIGN BY EVAN FEMINO.

FERALDOVE.COM

www.ingramcontent.com/pod-product-compliance
Lightning Source LLC
Chambersburg PA
CBHW081103300726
48976CB00011B/2708